LORD TRISTRAM'S LOVE MATCH

HER STERN HUSBAND BOOK THREE

R. R. VANE

Published by Blushing Books
An Imprint of
ABCD Graphics and Design, Inc.
A Virginia Corporation
977 Seminole Trail #233
Charlottesville, VA 22901

R. R. Vane
Lord Tristram's Love Match

Print ISBN: 978-1-63954-001-3
v1

CHAPTER 1

ENGLAND 1174

*F*rom the ramparts, Judith could already see the enemy steadily approaching, and right beside the symbol of Henry's rule, she glimpsed the azure banner which displayed a nimbly black eagle soaring with spread wings.

"My lady," Sir Roderick said in astonishment. "The banner... It's..."

Sir Roderick was in charge of the castle's defence, and there was now a look of deep worry in his eyes.

"I know what the banner is," Judith cut him off with an impatient wave of her hand. "How long can we last if there's a siege?"

"We're well prepared, my lady, and it could be perchance months. Redmore has strong defences and it is one of the few stone keeps in England. But–"

Sir Roderick paused, but Judith already knew what he meant to say. She nodded to herself, coming to see there was no other course. She had pledged her allegiance to the cause of Queen Eleanor and of her son, Young Henry, who had rebelled against their king together with two of his younger brothers. Nevertheless now Eleanor lay vanquished, and Redmore was one of the last places King Henry's loyal followers hadn't taken. Eleanor's cause was lost, so a siege would be pointless. The enemy would call for reinforcements and the castle would be eventually lost. And many lives would be wasted on both sides. Judith didn't think it fair that her people should die for her choices. They must not perish pointlessly just because their lady had chosen the side which had been vanquished in this war. Henry's victory had been arduous, because Eleanor and her sons had gathered many followers. Still, it was Henry who was victorious and not Eleanor's party.

"They will be upon us in less than an hour," Sir Roderick said, now casting expectant eyes upon his lady.

"You shall raise a white flag and open the gates," Judith answered in a steady voice.

She pulled her shoulders back, knowing too well there was no other course left. She prayed the enemy would prove merciful. Her fervent hope was that mercy would be given to her people. As for herself, she expected no mercy.

Sir Roderick looked relieved and nodded in acknowledgment of his lady's decision.

"I shall be there to meet them at the gates," Judith went on. "But I will need to speak to my lady mother. She does not know what I've resolved, and she needs to be told."

Sir Roderick bowed his head.

"Aye, my lady."

It was with a heavy heart that Judith made her way to the solar which her mother had turned into her chambers. Lady Fenice met her with an anguished look in her fine blue eyes.

"They're at our gates already? Our enemies?" she inquired.

Judith nodded.

"It's just as well then," her mother said, attempting to plaster a brave smile upon her face. "We shall withstand them. Redmore is strong and it will bear the siege. We've months and months ahead. And even if the castle's taken, we shall be able to take the secret escape tunnel your father built."

Judith knew the next words she would utter would be hard upon her mother. Yet her mother needed to be told the truth at once.

"I have decided to surrender," she said loud and clear.

"Surrender? Why? The castle stands strong."

"Yet our cause is lost. And the siege will end only with our defeat. They will send for more men. Redmore is one of the last castles King Henry hasn't taken. No one will aid us. Eleanor and her sons are vanquished. So there's no choice but to surrender."

"Are you so cowardly? It will be noble to fight to the end!" Lady Fenice countered with a regal tilt of her head.

"Noble, aye! Yet I cannot ask my people to sacrifice their lives over a noble cause. I cannot look them in the eye and tell them it's nobler to die for the sake of my honour," Judith countered in determined tones. "Father would not have wanted this, and you know it. He cared for his own, and, as his heir, I cannot do otherwise."

"They're only commoners," Lady Fenice muttered with a sigh.

Judith stared at her amazed, as she'd often been in these past months, she'd not been able to see before that her mother did not, in truth, care for the people put under their care. Yet it was so, and Judith tried to tell herself it was mainly the melancholy which had become lodged into her mother's soul which was causing this. Her mother had always been gentle and kind, and only of late had she started speaking so disparagingly of others.

"Mother, for all our sakes there is no choice but to surrender. We'll put ourselves at the mercy of our enemies, hoping they will prove gracious in their victory and spare our people."

Lady Fenice started to shake her head, but Judith halted her with a gesture.

"My mind is set and it is my decision to make, not yours."

At last, her mother bowed her head, clutching her heart.

"Perchance it is as you say. I am too frail of body. I cannot aid you in this."

"Take heart! No lord who holds his honour dear would dare harm a lady such as yourself!" Judith said, clasping her mother's hand.

Lady Fenice nodded with a tremulous smile on her beautiful face.

"Whose banner is the enemy under?" she asked at last, right before Judith could let herself out of the chamber.

Judith breathed in deep as she turned to face her mother yet again.

"De Brunne," she answered in a voice which only strived to seem steady.

"Ah," Lady Fenice muttered, and there was a long silence before she spoke again. "Daughter, I fear De Brunne will show you no mercy."

Judith summoned all the strength she could muster, telling herself not to dwell upon the past any longer.

"Yet he may show *you* mercy. And he will show my people mercy. It's all I ask," she said, and then hurried out of her mother's chamber, knowing time was growing short and that she needed to be at the gates when the enemy reached them.

It was not long before Redmore's gates were tossed open, to let in the conquering army of men who carried the azure banner with the eagle displayed. Judith stood there straight as an arrow, trying to still her thumping heart, as those who led the army rode in. There were two lord knights on horseback in their hauberks and helmets, accompanied by a man of the Church and the banner men. The lords dismounted, and they were both tall and broad of shoulders, yet one was leaner and slighter of form than the other. He walked to where she was with feline grace, as if the hauberk and helmet did not weigh heavy upon him. He spoke to her in a voice which sounded melodious, even in spite of its harsh tone. She knew that voice. She had no need of seeing the knight's face to know who he was. He was Tristram de Brunne, and both his face and voice had long haunted her dreams.

"It seems surrendering the castle is the only wise thing you ever did, *wife*," the voice uttered.

Wife. Judith straightened her spine even further, aware of the knights and soldiers now surrounding her and casting her looks of grim displeasure.

"*Sire*, if you recall, we are no longer wed," she said, striving to keep her dignity.

The lord knight didn't answer, but took the time to remove his helmet. He was, Judith noted when she looked better upon him, every bit as beautiful as she recalled him to be, even if his face was grimy with road dust and weary.

"You do not recall?" he flung at her in a bitter voice. "The Church did not agree to the annulment."

Judith stared at him, stunned. She had not known. Surely – the letter which had reached her more than one year ago had plainly stated that the Church had agreed on the annulment for which she'd petitioned. She'd read it herself. Many times. Then how had this come to be?

"Nay," she uttered shaking her head, but by the way Tristram was now looking upon her, it seemed he didn't believe she had not known of this.

The tall, wispy man of the Church came to stand by Tristram's side. He was not much older than Tristram, yet he wore a stern, disapproving expression upon his face, which nearly matched Lord de Brunne's hardened countenance. He spoke disdainfully to Judith, "The Church's word is law. You are still Lord Tristram's wife, my lady, and you're to receive heavy chastisement for the sins against your lord husband!"

Tristram halted the priest with a gesture.

"Cousin, we have decided it is upon me, and not upon the Church, to chastise my wife."

Wife. So she was still married to Tristram, although she'd been certain the annulment had been granted. But Judith was too distraught to care about what they were talking. It did not truly matter if she was still De Brunne's wife. She had already expected her fate would be dire, yet she had surrendered the castle so her people would be safe.

"The men and the women here, they surrendered freely. And they are not to be harmed!" she uttered, fighting hard to keep her voice from trembling.

"No one will harm them," Tristram replied tersely, beckoning his soldiers.

The way things unfolded then took place in a daze, as Judith watched the men who'd prepared to besiege her home make themselves masters of it. Yet, true to Lord Tristram's word, his soldiers behaved peacefully, as Sir Roderick and her own people met them with no opposition. Judith watched upon all this with relief, not caring what her own fate would be, and hoping her mother was still safely in the chambers where she'd closeted herself.

"Where is the lady Fenice?" Tristram asked, as if in echo of her thoughts, after his squires had helped him out of his hauberk.

"Please, do not harm my mother!" Judith pleaded, casting anguished glances at the grim priest and at the other man, a tall, broad-shouldered lord with brown hair about Tristram's own age.

The priest gave her a look of sheer disdain, and wanted to speak, but Tristram silenced him.

"She's ailing," Judith added, knowing she was not stating the full truth, however clinging to the hope her mother would escape the besiegers' wrath.

The priest scoffed, yet the other lord, whom Tristram had

earlier addressed as FitzRolf, said with a gracious bow of his head. "No honourable knight would harm an ailing woman. Besides, my lady, it is only you who has betrayed your allegiance to your husband. Lady Fenice is guilty only of standing against King Henry. And Henry has decided to show himself magnanimous to his foes, even if they erred against him. It is known to him that your mother is already ailing, so the lady shall be forgiven for her deeds."

Judith nodded in sheer relief. Her mother and her people were then safe. As for her own fate... She looked upon Tristram's hard, handsome face, and at once knew he would not be inclined to show her any mercy.

They were now in the inner bailey, and many eyes were upon them, when the priest spoke in a thundering voice for everyone to hear, "You've disobeyed your wedding vows! You have betrayed your husband!"

Tristram swiftly cut off the rest of the words the priest had meant to say, "'Tis best I deal with it. Here and now," he uttered grimly.

Judith had no time to understand what he meant by it. With widened eyes, she watched him beckon a squire and hand him the sword he'd refastened earlier on his hip after he'd shed his hauberk. With widened eyes still, she watched him as he calmly unbuckled his sword belt to the approving exclamations of his men. It took a while to understand why the men had begun to clamour in approval. She was still stunned when she felt Tristram's strong hand grab her by the arm. And then she shouted in more outrage than pain when Tristram's sword belt landed upon her bottom with a loud crack, although the outrage soon melted, overshadowed by the unexpected sting of the belt which began to fall upon her bottom again, and then again. And again. Judith tried to run away from the sheer sting of the belt, but her captor had a strong hold of her arm, as he was dragging her towards one of the wooden benches in the inner bailey. The belt kept landing with unfailing precision upon her behind and thighs, which soon began to burn as if stung by angry bees.

"Wait! I–" Judith tried to speak, but her punisher didn't heed any of her words.

The doubled sword belt he held in his hand was still busy sizzling her behind, and when they reached the bench, Judith was already feeling scalding tears of pain falling upon her cheeks. She'd never been given to easy tears, yet she couldn't help but succumb to them. Tristram forcefully dragged her across his lap, after seating himself on the bench, and Judith gritted her teeth to prevent herself from starting to sob. She tried to brace herself against the infernal sting of the accursed belt which she was certain would now land even more harshly upon her, and she vowed to herself she would be valiant until it was all over. However she'd not expected the sheer humiliation which followed. Her captor hoisted her skirts to expose her bare bottom to the approving cheers of the soldiers who were rejoicing in the punishment.

"Wait!" Judith found herself wailing, as she blushed in sheer mortification at the thought that not only Tristram's men, but her own people could now see her bare bottom and thighs which the belt must have already striped with angry red.

Soon she forgot to even feel humiliated as the doubled belt landed across her bare behind with a mightily loud crack. It hurt ten thousand times more to feel the belt upon her bare skin, and Judith no longer cared to hold back her tears. She cried. And then, when the belt cruelly caught the sensitive part of her sit spots, again and again, she simply started sobbing. As the accursed belt did its work, her whole bottom and upper thighs began to feel as if a blazing fire was burning there.

She was now weeping so hard, she only belatedly understood the demon who'd delivered her punishment had stopped at last, resting a battle-calloused hand on her scorched behind. Strangely, she felt a fire not only inside her bottom, but an unbearable heat inside her sex when he deigned to speak, in a hard, dispassionate voice, "Do you think you've learnt your lesson, wife?"

When she didn't swiftly answer, the accursed belt landed across the spot where her bottom met her thighs, and she could do nothing but sob, "Aye, husband!"

Blissfully, the demon seemed satisfied with her answer, but Judith's knees felt far too weak as he let her off his lap, after he'd straightened her skirts. He had to stand up and help support her, as she painfully tried to keep her balance. She'd never been spanked in her life, but now she understood why some of her childhood friends had feared their parents' punishment so much. The sting in her bottom was simply infernal, and she had to bite her lip hard, nearly tasting blood, in order to prevent herself from hopping from one foot to another. Instead, she just shifted her weight, trying to alleviate the sheer sting she now felt. The belting had mercifully stopped, yet she could still feel the fierce fire of it across her skin.

The jeers and laughter from Tristram's men stung nearly as much as her bottom, and through the haze of her tears, she could now perceive that even some of her own people had started smirking somewhat, callously finding amusement in her misery.

"'Tis done," Tristram tossed out, letting go of her arm, as it was obvious she could at last stand up by herself.

"Mild punishment," the priest scoffed, and Judith nearly shook her head in incredulity.

Mild? It didn't feel at all like mild punishment to her. In truth, she'd never felt as wretched in her life. Uncaring her gesture was unladylike, she simply wiped her teary face with the sleeve of her gown. She glowered at the demon who'd punished her, who, she noted, looked, as usual, nothing like a demon, but rather like an angel, with hair the colour of dark honey and long-lashed, brooding eyes. She felt disgusted with herself for noting his beauty at this very time. Her mother had been right then. Tristram de Brunne was indeed a fiend in spite of his angelic appearance.

"The punishment will suffice," Tristram flung grimly in his cousin's direction.

The priest glared and looked displeased, while the other knight gave a grave nod.

"It was a fair punishment," FitzRolf said.

Judith had a hard time holding her tongue, and she opened her mouth to protest, but a pointed look from Tristram made her clamp it shut. He was still holding the doubled belt in one hand, and she had no doubt he would make renewed use of it if she didn't hold her peace.

"Aye," Tristram tossed out at FitzRolf with a grim nod of his own. "Now that it's done and over with, we'll rest and break our fast."

He cast a telling glance in her direction, and she stared at him.

"Our men are hungry and weary," Tristram went on in that hard voice he employed of late. "You're still the lady of this house, aren't you?" he added pointedly.

She widened her eyes at him, barely able to comprehend. She'd already surrendered her home to him, which meant she now no longer held any status here. Unless he meant to keep her on as his wife. But this seemed incomprehensible to her. She'd spurned him and had sought an annulment of their marriage. And she'd chosen Eleanor's cause over Henry's. Surely, she could no longer be Tristram's wife or the lady of this house. She was now just a vanquished foe he meant to swiftly remove. Yet Tristram's dark eyes bored into her, making her focus on his words.

"Give orders, *wife*, and ready things for our rest and repast," Tristram called out sharply.

Judith breathed in deeply and decided to gather her thoughts later. It was now better to hurry to do her punisher's bidding.

Her tarrying or nursing her sore bottom would be to no avail. She was soon to learn what fate he had in store for her anyway, and at this time it seemed better to behave sensibly. Her pointless defiance would not help her people or her mother or, for that matter, herself. Striving hard to regain her composure and not to rub her blazing bottom, Judith proceeded to do her duty as the lady of the house, going to instruct the servants on what needed to be readied.

It was good to dwell upon menial chores, rather than on the sting in her behind and on the humiliation Tristram had bestowed upon her. Dame Berthe, who'd been responsible for most of the household duties, had passed away this winter due to a fever, and now these duties fell mainly upon Judith, since her mother's health and disposition were far too frail. In the past years, Judith had sought to learn these duties as well as she'd been able to, so now they came naturally to her. She now conferred with her people regarding the lodging and feeding of the men who'd come upon them. To Judith's relief, none of her people chose to ask how she fared after the punishment she'd received, and she felt grateful for it, finding it easier to forgive those who'd seemed to find a measure of entertainment in her spanking.

It was perhaps an hour later that things were ready for a meal, with benches and tables set in the Hall to accommodate each and every new man. Judith was loath to share the meal at the lord's table which she'd readied for Tristram and his peers, yet she had no choice but to comply when her husband beckoned her by his side, making it all too plain he was still her lord.

"Sit, wife," he bid, not even deigning to look at her.

Judith tried to sit down, but jolted upright due to the fierce sting in her behind. It seemed Sir Tristram's belt had done an even more thorough job than she'd thought.

"I'd rather stand, my lord," she said with a heartfelt glower.

The laughter which reverberated around her made her blush

crimson, as Tristram's men began to make merry over the chastisement the lady of the house had received. Even the dour priest gave a malicious grin, but Tristram didn't laugh or smile.

"Was that defiance I saw in your eyes, wife?" Tristram asked, his voice was steely.

Judith straightened her shoulders.

"What do you wish me to say?" she countered, feeling truly weary of what had gone on today.

"She's still defiant," the priest cut in, with a look of sheer disdain. "'Tis obvious you should cast her away and send her to a convent for her treachery. It is the only course left."

Judith simply shuddered at the words, imagining harsh scissors cutting away her long hair, which she'd always thought her one glory. She imagined grey walls, stifling silence, and joyless prayer. Was this the fate Tristram had in store for her? She stared at him with undisguised anger in her eyes. Tristram didn't miss her look.

"Perchance you wish me to teach you another lesson here and now, wife," he said as their gazes locked.

She now openly glared at him, no longer caring what would happen to her. It was the other knight's voice, the one called FitzRolf, which cut in pointedly, "My Lord De Brunne, perhaps you and your wife should settle this in private."

Judith could only feel grateful this lord would spare her the humiliation of another public spanking. But her heart started thumping in anguish when Tristram took his friend's advice and grabbed her by the arm, leading her to the stairs, and then to her bedchamber. He knew very well where her bedchamber was. After all, they'd shared it for the brief time he'd resided in her home. Judith recalled those times, and she recalled a Tristram who had behaved very differently from the grim, forceful knight he'd now proven himself to be. When they reached her chamber, he swiftly closed the door behind them, and Judith fully expected him to take her over his knee again. She cast him a defiant look, vowing to bite her tongue rather than succumb to new tears when he spanked her.

Nevertheless, Tristram made no gesture after he sat himself in a chair. Instead he talked, in that hard voice he'd used all day, "We both know you've betrayed me, but we are still wed, in spite of your endeavours to undo our match. The Church and the King urge me to cast you aside and force you to join a convent. Your home and lands will be mine by rights, since you've no kin on your father's side they could revert to. Besides, you have surrendered them yourself. Now Redmore will be secure and will become a stronghold against Henry's enemies."

Judith closed her eyes in weariness. She should have expected this, since there seemed to be no other course open to her. She'd not thought herself married to Tristram any longer, but the Church's ruling had made her into both a sinner and a traitor. Since they were still wed, she was formally guilty of standing not only against the King, but also against her husband.

"However," Tristram added, "no law in this world forbids a husband from seeking reconciliation with an estranged wife. Since we are still wed, no man, even a king or a priest, can over-rule my word in this. You could remain here, as the lady of this house and as my lady."

Judith opened her eyes in sheer surprise.

"In spite of everything, you would be willing to keep me as your wife?" she asked with raised eyebrows.

"Aye. As my *chastened*, *repentant* wife," Tristram said stressing words which made Judith purse her lips in sheer anger.

She had spurned him by seeking to end their marriage—that was true. Yet she'd not betrayed him in any way. She had not meant to stand against him. It was just the decision of supporting Eleanor's cause against Henry's which she'd made. It was a decision several other noble families had made, and that Judith understood she would make again, because she believed Eleanor's cause to be right. Nevertheless, Eleanor's supporters had been defeated and Henry now kept her imprisoned. Judith assumed most of Eleanor's vanquished followers had been punished with exile or even death. So she supposed Tristram's offer was gracious, but she couldn't help feeling anger at the disdainful way he spat the word *chastened*. The fierce sting in her behind made her go over the hard spanking she'd received in front of all to see.

Tristram must have perceived the anger in her eyes, because he laughed mirthlessly. "A bleak choice for you, my lady, is it not? Joining a convent or staying on as my wife. As I recall, being my wife seemed to you a fate worse than death, did it not?"

Judith avoided looking at him, because she fully recalled how it had been between them. And she did not want to think upon what had been. She strived to look only upon the present time. Two choices then. Both bleak.

Tristram went on savagely, with a disdainful wave of his hand, "Not that you deserve it, but I'll give you a third choice. You and your mother could escape in the deep of the night, and I'll bid my men tell they haven't seen you. Your mother has kin in Aquitaine. So you could head for Dover and find a ship. And you'll be free of me, just as you've always wished."

Judith thought of her mother, and of how her mother had always hated this cold land.

"What of our vows? You said we are still wed."

Tristram shook his head with a mocking smile on his lips.

"I'll ask for an annulment. And something tells me the Church will be inclined to grant it *this time*."

The sunny picture of Aquitaine was however replaced by the image of her home in Judith's mind. Redmore was her home. And she'd always loved it fiercely.

"So you'll have me leave my home in the dead of the night as if I were a thief. This is my home! And you're the thief!" she cried in a high voice, not caring he'll make good on his threat and give her another spanking right here and now.

"It *was* your home, which you lost through your own treachery. You've just surrendered it and it is rightfully and honourably mine. And you…"

He paused with a twist of those sinfully beautiful lips.

"You are mightily lucky I'm still willing to suffer you as my wife," he added at last, staring away from her in sheer disdain.

Judith hated the word *suffer* just as much as she'd hated it when he'd spoken of her as *chastened*. Yet she raked a hand through her hair understanding the choices before her were clear. Life entombed in a convent. Escape to a new land, leaving behind everything she'd known. Or a life of bleak servitude in her former home, on Tristram's sufferance. All were hard choices.

"Your wife…" she found herself repeating with a shake of her head.

"Aye. *Mine*. To share my bed as a proper wife should. To do as I see fit, and be chastened for disobedience whenever I see fit."

Judith had the urge of instantly rubbing her scorched bottom. The manner in which Tristram had chastened her today left no room for doubt he had sound punishments in store for her. It was hard to reconcile the picture of the hard, grim warrior who'd spanked her with his sword belt with that of the gentle, courteous knight who had slept chastely by her side in those first days of their marriage. She had not allowed him to bed her, even if he had been within his rights to do so, and he had not pressed for it. He had not forced her to lie with him. But things had changed, and she had no doubt now he'd demand what he had graciously refrained from taking. She thought of sharing her body with Tristram, and blushed fiercely, understanding, like so many times before, that this was a part of their marriage she'd have no difficulty complying with. As always, she lusted after him, even after the hard spanking he'd given her today.

"Your wife," she repeated, dumbly, striving to hate this man for what he'd done to her.

Tristram said nothing, and Judith frantically wondered, like so many times before, if she'd ever managed to fully hide from him the scorching lust she felt whenever she glanced upon his beautiful form.

She reasoned there was no helping it. A convent was the last place where she wanted to spend her life, and Aquitaine was an uncertain choice and an arduous journey for her mother. Most of all, she could never leave her people. With her father gone, they depended upon her. She just couldn't leave them at the mercy of the man who'd nearly set siege to her castle.

"I-I choose to stay," she muttered almost inaudibly.

Tristram raised his dark eyebrows, which were, just like his eyes, in such strange yet pleasing contrast with his fair hair.

"I would have you state it loud and clear," he uttered in a tone which left no doubt who held the advantage in this arrangement.

Judith suppressed a sigh. It was, she tried to tell herself, the only choice she had left.

"I shall be your wife," she said resolutely, knowing this was a bond she would no longer be able to undo.

"There's no return from it. And I will have no more false pledges or treachery from you," Tristram told her in a hard voice.

In silence, they returned to the Hall, to join the table, and Judith tried to hold her head high and her back straight, knowing all eyes were upon her and recalling they'd witnessed her deep humiliation.

"Strive to look repentant!" Tristram hissed to her between his teeth right before they reached the high table.

"Whatever for?" Judith couldn't help saying venomously. "Besides I am certain you already plan to teach me repentance later."

"That I do," Tristram retorted softly, taking hold of her arm and leading her to the table.

Judith began to fear he would truly spank her anew, right there at the table in front of all to see, just as callously as he'd done before, but he only made her sit by his side, on the hard wooden bench. Judith winced at the pain in her rear as she did so, but the pain seemed somewhat lesser than earlier. It was uncomfortable to sit down, yet she could bear it. So she bore it, resolving not to give Tristram or any of the men at the table the chance to see her eyes fill with tears.

Tristram's cousin, the churchman who was called Isidore, instantly perceived she meant to defy them.

"Your wife doesn't look chastened to me."

"Desist. She has already been punished today," Tristram said quietly, taking a sip of wine from the goblet which lay in front of him.

There were displeased mutters from several of the men in the Hall, who, Judith thought in rancour, were without doubt keen on witnessing her further humiliation.

"Her eyes are dry of tears, and she stares upon us haughtily," Isidore persisted, casting Judith a glance meant to thwart her.

"I have already vowed to school her to obedience. And I shall certainly make it my purpose. Now can I eat in peace?" Tristram flung out.

Isidore frowned in return.

"Her head's uncovered. She looks like a loose woman!"

Judith's long black hair was fashioned in a simple long plait which she wore upon one shoulder. Of late she had become used to wearing it like this again, since she'd considered herself an unmarried woman and it had been simpler not to wear a wimple. But Isidore plainly took her uncovered hair as a sign of her sinful behaviour and of the way he thought she'd spurned her marriage vows. In churchmen's eyes it was shameful for married women not to cover their hair.

17

Tristram shrugged, as if he was not greatly concerned by the priest's words, and Judith painfully recalled him telling her once that her black hair looked wondrous and that it was a shame to cover it. She gritted her teeth, striving not to dwell upon the past, but only on the present moment. At present, Tristram was speaking in a level voice.

"Rest assured, cousin. My lady wife is bound to learn only too well what is expected of her."

Isidore arched an eyebrow, but under Tristram's steady gaze, he reluctantly refocused his attention on his own meal. Judith stared at the trencher in front of her, recalling she hadn't had a morsel to eat today, but knowing she wouldn't be able to force a single bite down her throat. Yet her husband wouldn't let her be.

"Eat. Now. I say," he commanded her in a terse voice which left no room to wonder what he would do if she didn't comply with his command right now.

Was this what her life with her husband would always be from now on? This life with this new and different Tristram? But perchance Tristram had always been like this – willing to completely rule over her – and she'd not been able to see it before. Judith stifled a sigh and she willed herself to chew on a chunk of bread. However it was not for fear of Tristram's punishment that she was forcing herself to eat, but rather because she knew she would feel ill and faint later this evening if she didn't. She forced herself to take the morsel of meat on Tristram's knife, which he had cut for her.

"Thank you, my lord," she muttered in a sullen voice, making her ungracious tone at odds with her gracious words.

His dark eyes looked daggers at her.

"I've given you a kind reprieve, but soon I shall cure you of your defiant ways," he said grimly, and his words rang loud, for all to hear.

Judith strived to make herself ignore the deep feeling of shame she still harboured about the way he'd chastened her.

CHAPTER 2

Sheer relief coursed through Judith's veins when later Tristram allowed her to go and look upon her mother in the solar. Judith did that without tarrying, knowing her mother would be anguished and would want to know what had occurred upon Redmore's surrender. Yet the exhaustion of the day had obviously taken its toll, and Lady Fenice was already asleep at this early hour when Judith stepped in. Judith allowed herself a while to sit down on her sore bottom and simply gather her thoughts, ensconced in the privacy of her mother's quarters.

It was plain Tristram now hated her, and he had cause for it, since she had indeed spurned and humiliated him by seeking an annulment of their marriage. And it was plain he meant to make her life an ordeal for it from now on, but Judith knew if she were to make her choice again, she would still say *aye* to his offer. She loved Redmore and her people, and could not ever picture her life elsewhere. So she supposed she should give her prayers of thanks for having been allowed to remain in her home. She strived not to think at all of what Tristram must have in store for her tonight when she finally regained her bedchamber, where she already supposed he would be waiting for her.

Tristram was indeed there, and by his wet, darkened hair, and by the tub which still lay in the chamber, she understood he'd already taken his bath. He was now dressed in a fresh undyed undertunic, and one of his squires was already taking away the clothes his lord had worn today.

"I bid the servants to empty the tub and bring fresh warm water for you," Tristram said, not looking at her.

"Oh, so now you're to command me even when I should have a bath?" Judith couldn't help saying.

He still didn't look at her when he spoke again, in a voice which was hard and dispassionate, and Judith recalled that, until today, she'd never thought Tristram's beautiful voice could ever sound hard.

"The water will soothe your sore bottom."

Judith felt like strangling him.

"I thank you for your tender care. Would it that you had shown the same tender care when you were attending to the same bottom earlier in the bailey!"

"That was indeed tender care," Tristram retorted with a cocked eyebrow. "The tender care of a husband for his miscreant wife."

He'd always had a way with words, the fiend, Judith mused to herself, but she decided to take his advice. A warm bath was a gift which should never be refused, and perchance he was right, and it might soothe her reddened skin.

Yet she recalled he was in the chamber, and he had no plan of leaving it. She also distinctly recalled he'd told her he now expected her to share his bed. And she had said *aye* to the bargain which he'd offered. Still, after the servants fulfilled their duties and made their retreat, Judith lingered in front of the tub. A serving girl had untied the laces at the back of her bliaut, and had helped her remove both her *cors* and her long *girone*. She was now standing only in her underdress in front of the bathtub, knowing that once she removed it, she would be naked in a chamber where she was now alone with her husband. Perchance she should strive to bathe in this garment, as she knew some of the ladies of her acquaintance usually did.

Tristram must have perceived her hesitation. He tossed out at her in a mocking voice, "I've never known water to bite anyone. But by the way you're now staring at it, I'm certain you believe it can bite you."

She didn't dignify his mocking comment with an answer, but decided she had sealed her own fate when she'd agreed to stay on as Tristram de Brunne's wife. There was no point in playing the shrinking, modest maiden now, so she decided not to care for modesty and to remove the shift. After she'd done so, she cast a furtive glance in Tristram's direction to see if he was looking upon her, but Tristram seemed busy with the task of sorting out the bundle of his belongings which one of his squires had brought, and of settling them in one of the chests in her chamber. Judith told herself she should feel relieved he wasn't looking upon her, but after a while she began to feel simply irked he was so pointedly ignoring her.

In all fairness though, Judith soon discovered the fiend had had the right of it. The warm water, which was tepid and not hot, was like a balm upon her scorched bottom, and after she was done bathing and drying herself, and slipped into a fur-lined robe, she started feeling better than she had the whole day. Once the servants took the tub away, she and Tristram were once again left alone in the bedchamber, and Judith became even more keenly aware of what he'd told her about their marriage.

She waited for a while for him to look upon her, but as he didn't, she sighed and decided to break the silence. "What now?" she asked in a weary voice.

Tristram at last deigned to glance upon her. He said nothing though, just staring at her with those dark eyes of his. He strode to the bed and sat himself on it, but he made no other gesture.

"You said you now expect me to share your bed," Judith said

bluntly, knowing there was no return from what she'd agreed to. "I vowed to do so. And here I am."

Still, Tristram said nothing and he did not make a single move to come to where she was.

"Fine," Judith said in a relieved voice. "Then I shall sleep if you want none of me."

It was perchance best he meant to spurn her. She did feel weary. And, in spite of the warm bath, her bottom still felt quite sore from his spanking.

"So," Tristram said softly. "I see you're still foresworn."

Judith instantly bristled at the word.

"I mean to keep my word! As for betraying you before, I…"

He halted her with a gesture.

"I do not care to hear your prattle. You promised to lie with me as my wife. Or have you changed your mind?"

Deep heat clung to Judith's cheeks.

"I haven't!" she vowed, squaring her shoulders.

Silence fell between them, yet Tristram seemed in no hurry to stride to her and do what he professed he wanted.

"Just claim me then! I will not fight you!" Judith flung at him, now at the end of her tether.

Tristram smiled mockingly and did not make a single gesture, simply cocking a dark eyebrow at her. And Judith suppressed a deep sigh within herself. She now knew how things stood. They stood exactly as her husband wanted them. He would not woo her. And he would not ravish her. This meant she had only one course left if she wanted to have this marriage stand.

She strode to him, pausing in front of him uncertainly. He didn't move. It was plain he wished to humiliate her, by leaving her no choice but to woo him.

"How should I do this?" she asked, attempting to make her voice calm and dispassionate. "Will you not help me in that at least?"

"Why should I help you? Were you of any help when I attempted to woo you?" he countered pointedly.

Judith's cheeks blushed fiercely, because she recalled only too well the last time they'd shared this chamber and this bed. Tristram had courted her with tantalizing kisses and caresses and she'd been sinfully tempted to lie with him, her lawful husband, but at the last moment she'd rejected him. And, chivalrously, he hadn't pressed on, although she understood it must have been hard for him to restrain himself.

"Fine," she muttered between gritted teeth. "I suppose I should undress you first."

She attempted to reach for his long undertunic, but he pushed her hand away.

"No need of it. This tunic stays on. It's just my cock you need to tend to."

Judith blushed to the roots of her hair. The Tristram she'd known would never have used coarse words like this. It was plain she'd not known the true Tristram. Her mother had then been right in her advice. And Judith herself had been right to want to put an end to their marriage. Yet now she had agreed to have it stand.

"If you care for my advice in this, I think it best *you* should undress," Tristram further taunted her, with the same mocking smile on his sinfully beautiful lips.

"Fine, then I will," Judith found herself retorting. "No longer am I the shy, tongue-tied and simple girl I was when we first wed!"

"So then you must have already perceived I am no longer the soft, foolish man I was," Tristram said in return, looking at her levelly.

Judith decided to pay him no mind. She angrily peeled off her robe, and went to stand in front of her husband fully naked.

"There. I have complied with your command. What next?" she asked in a vexed voice, but found herself blushing more fiercely than before as Tristram's dark eyes roamed unashamedly over the curves of her body.

She struggled to still her thumping heart and withstand his perusal, and she bit hard into her lip at his next words.

"Your breasts and hips are fuller than last time we met," he told her and his voice no longer sounded harsh or mocking.

Judith knew herself not to be beautiful, and now she assumed she might appear to him even less so than she'd been years ago. And he might wish to humiliate her by disparaging her appearance. Yet the way he'd spoken the words, and his dark, liquid eyes which were now staring upon her seemed to hold lust rather than contempt.

"You are to touch yourself for me," Tristram now commanded, but his voice was full of heat and it didn't sound like a harsh command at all.

His voice had always been compelling, and Judith found herself unwittingly reaching to touch the peaks of her breasts, which, she found, had already stirred under the cool air of the room.

"Like so?" she muttered questioningly, because, in truth, she'd never touched herself like this even when she was alone in her chamber, and now she was doing it in front of the man she'd always lusted after.

"Aye," Tristram acquiesced watching with avid eyes as Judith's palms brushed over her nipples in slow circles.

And soon Judith began to feel a sweet ache not only in her nipples, but also in her quim. It was a stab of piercing desire which made her half-close her eyes and bite even deeper into her plump lower lip. Tristram, the fiend, seemed to sense what it was that she now fiercely craved to do.

"Now touch your quim, wife. Stroke the secret spot of it until it begins to blossom."

How did he already know of that hidden part of her body? Judith had never imagined a man might know of the secret place within a woman's quim. It was a place she'd often touched when she'd thought of him in her lonely bed, feeling shameful and sinful each time after she'd done so, but unable to stop herself from doing it. And now as she obeyed Tristram's command, she found it did not feel at all shameful to do it in front of him.

"Good," Tristram said softly after a long while, when Judith understood she was already gushing wet and burning to touch *him*.

He simply pulled at his long undertunic, to release a long cock which stood perfectly erect in front of her.

"Ah," Judith said, biting even harder into her bottom lip. "This... How do I..."

Blushing fiercely, she drew close to him and stroked the length of him rather artlessly. She'd heard men liked it when a woman touched their rod. But her mother had kept her mostly sheltered from servants' talk, so she didn't know much more than this. Still, she loved the feel of him as she began to stroke him – all soft velvety skin sheathing hard muscle. When she looked upon Tristram's face, she found his dark eyes even darker than before. His own teeth were digging into his bottom lip and his breathing was laboured. He most certainly liked this. And Judith suppressed a triumphant smile as she decided to become even bolder than she'd been. She did what she had always pictured in her mind she would do. She straddled him and she simply rubbed herself against him, allowing him to feel the hot wetness of her quim as she did so.

Yet, lightning fast, Tristram now switched positions. Judith soon found herself lying on her back as he pinned her arms above her head with one of his battle-calloused hands. His other hand came between them, to stroke her quim with clever fingers. And it was not long before Judith's nether parts began to feel even wetter. Now she was gushing and she felt deeply ashamed he was for certain able to see her sheer want of him.

Tristram's beautifully sculpted lips twisted in a cruel smile.

"So wet, wife. Wet for my thrust," he said softly.

Judith squirmed in both pleasure and pain beneath his body. She frantically wished him to thrust inside her. And her well spanked, red behind could hardly bear the touch of the bed beneath her. So it was both in pain and anticipated pleasure that she now raised her hips to him, but the fiend wouldn't do the deed. Instead he perused her with his dark, brooding eyes.

"Tell me this, wife mine," he said in a silky voice. "How come that when we last shared the bed you flinched from me and now you're so wet and eager for my cock?"

He rubbed himself against her, letting his hard cock brush against her wetness, and the heat in both her sex and her sore bottom became maddening.

"I…" Judith muttered, with her cheeks turning crimson at the words he'd uttered, although he'd stated the plain truth.

"I'll have no more deceit from you. So tell me how this strange thing came to be. Why are you so wet and eager now when years before you were fearful of my touch?"

"I…"

Judith knew there was now no return from it. She had resolved to be truthful to him. And it would only make things worse if she attempted to deceive him as she had years ago.

"I lied," she muttered, as pain as sharp as a splinter began to pierce her heart.

It was a truth she'd vainly tried to push away from her mind in this past year. It was a pain which had lingered inside her and which she'd attempted to ignore. She'd always wanted Tristram fiercely, in spite of everything and in spite of her mother's dire warnings.

"Lied?" Tristram echoed in that voice of his, which was just as beautiful as the rest of him.

"Lied. Yes. I lied to you. I never was uneager," Judith muttered in sheer misery.

"Lying should never go unpunished," Tristram said and his voice held both heat and menace in it. "Don't you think?"

Then he did something which drove Judith even more frantic than before. He licked the side of her neck, trailing his hot breath upon her skin as he did so, and stroking the scorched lips of her quim with clever fingers. She nearly swooned with longing, and muttered in incoherent acquiescence, "Y-yes..."

"Good. And what do you think the punishment for lying should be, wife?" he asked, as his free hand had now begun to rub the sweet spot between her legs which had already swollen with deep desire.

"Ah..." Judith had a hard time speaking coherently.

He stopped his ministrations.

"So?" he asked cruelly.

"S-spank me?" Judith made herself say, although her poor scorched bottom tingled fiercely just upon uttering the words.

"A worthy thought," Tristram acquiesced, as he brought back his hand to tend to her quim.

The pleasure returned, fierce, yet the sting in her bottom reminded her how soundly Tristram had chastened her. Did he mean to spank her now, even when her bottom was still blazing from his earlier spanking? As if in echo of her thoughts, Tristram said softly, "Never fear, I shall chasten you. But later. Now I have other things upon my mind."

He thrust one finger inside her, gently probing her wet folds.

"A maiden, still?" he asked after a while, and his voice was incredulous.

Judith's eyebrows rose in sheer surprise. Surely, he knew he was the only man she'd wed, and she'd not let him bed her.

Tristram's finger was soon replaced with his long cock which simply slid inside her, causing her to wince in pain. The pain was fleeting though, and she soon found herself becoming accustomed to his hard length stretching her wet passage.

"A maiden now no longer," Tristram muttered, as he began to move inside her.

At first he slid in and out of her slowly and gently, as if wanting her to get used to him. Then Judith came to welcome his thrusts and wanted more of them. She raised her hips to him eagerly, spurred not only by the soreness in her bottom, but by the fierce ache in her sex. She wanted so much more of him, but she noted in deep surprise, Tristram's hard cock had now withdrawn from her body. He sat up with a firm, determined look in his dark eyes.

"Wife, I now want you to beg me for it," he said in a voice which was both hard and hot.

Judith suppressed a curse on her lips. She'd never felt this way. The mixture of pain and pleasure was simply maddening. And now he was set on torturing her.

"Beg me to thrust inside you, wife," Tristram commanded.

He was obviously more master of himself than she was, Judith thought, fiercely hating both him and herself for what she uttered next.

"Please, husband," she muttered, despising the pleading in her voice.

"Please, what?" her tormentor echoed softly, coming to rub his stiff cock against her wet, inflamed sex.

"Please, come inside me," Judith begged.

He cursed under his breath, as he grabbed her hips and plunged himself inside her, deeper and fiercer than before. The world seemed to melt around Judith, and there was only him and the hard length of his cock. She lost all sense of time, and it seemed to her it was her wedding night, that night long ago when she'd become bound to Tristram. At the time, she'd been incredulous a man like Tristram would ever want to bind himself to a woman like her. And now he was inside her – closer to her than any being in this world had ever been. He was and for a moment she came to believe he was entirely hers, but she understood it was not so and it could never be so.

Judith came back to herself only when she felt Tristram's hot, sticky seed between her legs. He collapsed next to her, and she sat up, no longer caring for the pain in her spanked bottom as she did so. There was an ache now throbbing between her legs, but Judith understood this was because he'd taken her maidenhead tonight. The ache was bearable, and far less uncomfortable than the sting in her behind.

"You should clean yourself," Tristram said coldly, now propping himself on one elbow, and raking his hand through his tousled fair hair.

Judith did as he'd told her, soon making use of the cloth and bowl of fresh water which lay on the table in the chamber. She was aware that as she did so, Tristram's dark eyes roamed upon her form, resting upon her bottom, which must be still striped with red from his belt. She strived to ignore his bold, masterful gaze, reasoning she'd have to brace herself for her new life with a man who now despised her.

"Come here," Tristram ordered her, patting the bed. She chafed under the command, but she obeyed him because there was no choice for her any longer.

He made her lie on her belly, and Judith thought she'd die of mortification when he began to slide his palm against her well chastened behind.

"Still red, and warm to the touch," he said in his silky, melodious voice. "A job well done, wife, don't you think?" he added mockingly.

Judith stifled a curse on her lips. Strangely, the touch of his rough, warrior's hand on her bottom didn't bring pain, but, rather, a peculiar, delicious ache. When she tarried to answer his mocking question, he gave her bottom a swat, and she bit her lip, stunned by the way the faint sting of his touch mingled with hot pleasure. He'd given her the belt today. Hard. And now she should resent both his touch and his talk of punishment.

She heaved a deep sigh, striving to recall herself. "You punished me hard, and you know it. You're obviously rejoicing I'm now at your mercy. Is this why you decided not to force me to join a convent? Because you want to have your vengeance upon me?" she said, unable to stop herself from asking this of him outright.

"Certainly," Tristram acquiesced. "Why else would I have kept you as my wife?"

There was an odd, strained note in his voice she belatedly caught, but she dismissed it. He was entitled to his pride and she knew her petition for an annulment of their marriage had deeply humiliated him. She'd asked for an annulment on grounds of non-consummation, because, in truth, they had not shared their bodies. Yet it had not been that Tristram had been unable to consummate the marriage. She'd not brought herself to lie with him and he had not forced himself upon her. And... She sighed, knowing he now felt entitled to his revenge. Still, it was strange a man as handsome and well-born as he would choose to keep a wife who'd spurned and humiliated him. Fear started to clutch her heart, as a thought came upon her.

"You do not mean to cast me aside now, do you? Trick me into lying with you just to prove you can have me, and then toss me into a convent?"

Her heart thumped fiercely in the deep silence which followed.

"That would be cruel vengeance, wouldn't it?" Tristram said at last, with a careless laugh.

Judith had a sickening feeling in the pit of her stomach.

"But, wife of mine, you need to stop judging me by your own measure," he added in a voice which sounded fully disdainful.

His palm began to slide in tantalizing circles over Judith's sore bottom, and she had to strive hard to keep her head clear as she weighed upon what he'd said.

"To set your mind at ease," Tristram went on. "I have no treachery whatsoever in mind."

He swatted her bottom as he said it, harder than before, and Judith felt a stab of ignoble pleasure in her sex just at the same time as the sting of his slap. It had been a mild spank, but her bottom was still very tender from the belting she'd received at his hand not six hours before.

"I am weary," Tristram let her know in an arrogant voice. "So I'll postpone your punishment. It shall be done tomorrow."

Judith told herself she should hate him for his obvious enjoyment of having her at his mercy, and for punishing her so callously today. She strived to tell herself her mother had been right all along, and Tristram would truly end up making her life wretched. Hadn't he admitted, as much himself now, that he meant to make her life wretched?

CHAPTER 3

ristram sighed deeply, casting a frowning glance upon the woman who'd already fallen asleep by his side, on her belly, with her deliciously striped bottom on full display. His cock stirred, and both anger and lust mingled inside him. So he finally had the truth of it. Those years ago he'd held his lust at bay, because he'd thought Judith was unprepared for his touch. He'd honourably kept his distance, not wanting to bed an unwilling woman, although she'd pledged herself to him. But it turned out his wife hadn't been unwilling. The heat with which she'd loved him tonight had told him plainly he now had the truth of it. In the past he'd thought to give her time to get adjusted to him, but it now seemed plain, by the unrestrained way in which she'd loved him, that she lusted for him just as much as he lusted for her. Why then had she sought an annulment? He had been unable to understand her actions and also unable to grant the annulment. Neither Henry nor the prelates of Henry's choosing had given him a choice. And now... He raked a hand through his hair, not knowing why all those years ago she'd spurned him as she had, and recalling that once he'd sought to earn her love.

FOUR YEARS AGO, 1170, London

IT WAS upon a morning that Tristram heard a voice which he would never in his life forget. It came from the garden of the royal palace, and it was the warmest, most enticing voice Tristram had ever heard. Whenever he'd conjured up mermaids in his mind, he'd thought their voices would sound just like this. The song was sung in Occitan, not Norman, yet Tristram could understand it. His ancestors were Norman and did not come from the South of France like those of Eleanor, and of those courtiers loyal to her, but he soon caught the feel and the rhythm of the song, and he found its words strangely beautiful. The song was of the love between Tristan and his Yseult, and of the honeysuckle which was a symbol of their love which was called a *chevrefoil*. Tristram had heard the song of the *chevrefoil* often sung by the *trouveres* and troubadours of the court, but he'd never heard it sung quite like this. The tune and words were different and strange – warmer and more melodious than any song he'd heard in either Norman or Occitan.

Unable to stop, Tristram made his way towards the place where the voice was coming from, compelled to learn who was singing. Unfortunately the singing stopped well before he was able to reach the spot from which the sounds had reverberated, and when he finally arrived, there was no one there, and all he could stare at was a bush of briar roses. Upon a whim, he plucked one briar rose which he kept in his hand when he went to meet his best friend for sword practice.

"You're already daydreaming, I see," his friend, Bertran Fitz-Rolf, told him with a smile when they at last set eyes upon each other.

Tristram smiled in return.

"I was dreaming of beauty. Of a voice I heard coming from the garden. A woman's voice, uncanny!"

FitzRolf laughed.

"And now you're thinking this unknown woman should be as beautiful as her voice."

"Yes," Tristram said, then laughed in turn. "No... I don't know. Does it matter? Who will care even if her face is plain when her voice is so uncannily beautiful?"

"Of course, you would say so. Beside your sword, you care for naught but songs and stories," his friend told him with a shake of his head.

"They are the best thing in this world," Tristram replied, still musing upon his mysterious woman.

Her voice had sounded mesmerizing, yet young, and he distinctly recalled all the timbres of the voices of the women he'd met at Court. He'd always had a keen ear he prided himself in. This woman was someone he didn't know. A noblewoman of Occitan ancestry, who was newly come to Court. And in the next days he eagerly waited to come upon her, but he didn't chance to perceive her. It was only when he was beginning to think the whole thing had been a strange dream of his, that he had occasion to meet her one day.

It was the month of May, one filled with court entertainments, and this leisure day was one of joyous games which were well loved by the ladies and lords of the court. Tristram had always been an avid game player, and he'd grown up with three sisters. Unlike those knights who spurned the tamer, gentler games ladies enjoyed, he found great entertainment in such pastimes. Besides, he loved good-natured flirting, and thought most knights were foolish not to want to share diverting jests and joyous games with women. So he agreed to play a game of blindman's bluff with good cheer when one of the ladies asked him.

"I'm the best at this," he warned the lady laughingly, as she was tying the blindfold across his eyes. "And I'll guess each and every one of you."

"We'll see," the lady answered with a laugh of her own. "You said each and every one of us, remember?"

"I did," Tristram answered, because he knew all the ladies in this game and he had no trouble recognizing a familiar voice, even when its possessor whispered or tried to distort it.

There was some laughter and low mutters from the ladies, and some feet shuffling around him, and Tristram waited patiently for the first lady to call his name.

"Come on," he urged teasingly. "I'll prove myself to you once again, although you know that, in this game, I've never been beaten."

Nevertheless he simply stirred at the voice who next called his name. It was, certainly, a voice he already knew, but he didn't know the name or face of the lady who'd spoken. It was his mysterious mermaid.

"Tristram," the voice called out, and he simply loved the way his name reverberated in the garden.

"You've cheated, my ladies," he said, as his heart skipped a beat. "I've never met the lady who's called my name, and you already know it. It is unfair to bring a lady who wasn't even in the game."

He felt loath to remove his blindfold, even when several of the ladies conceded with exaggerated sighs they'd only tried to jest with him. Something inside him had been deeply moved and he did not wish to feel disappointed when he at last met the woman who had the most enticing voice in this world. When one of the ladies at last untied the blindfold, he glanced around him, seeking to see the woman who'd spoken. His eyes soon found her, the only unfamiliar face among the ladies now in the game. Her face was not, indeed, even half as beautiful as her voice, but he found his gaze roaming appreciatively on the ample curves of her body. And when he looked the second time upon her face, he found he already liked it, although it didn't meet the canons of courtly beauty he'd been taught to set store on.

"I'm Tristram, as you already know, my lady," he said boldly. "But I've not had the pleasure of learning your name."

"It's... Judith," she replied, and her voice was a mere whisper when she spoke.

She seemed ill at ease among the ladies, and it appeared she'd been brought in the game rather reluctantly. Tristram soon found she was shy, and unused to courtly games and teasing, so he didn't press upon her. Still, her voice just lingered in his mind during the next days, and he discovered he couldn't get it out of his mind. And he not only thought of her voice, but of her, as she'd seemed so different and so apart from the ladies of his acquaintance. She had large, watchful eyes, and had just listened to the others' talk, rather than hurrying to join in it. But, Tristram recalled, she'd been well spoken and polite whenever someone had chanced to address her. *Judith*. She lingered in his mind, and he even found himself asking his mother about her upon a day when they shared a meal at their London home.

"Judith of Redmore," his mother said and nodded.

"An English name, Northern by the sound of it," Tristram mused. "I thought she was Occitan."

"Her mother's family is. Fenice de Fael was her name before she wed an English lord from the North. But you already know Judith's aunt – Edith, who's lady-in-waiting whenever the Queen comes back to our English court."

Tristram frowned in displeasure. The lady Edith was the worst gossip at Court. Perchance her niece had inherited the same penchant for gossip. He strove to shrug away the thought of Judith, because, after all, she was just a young woman he'd chanced upon.

"Why are you asking?" her mother asked with a shrewd glance.

"Never you mind," he replied, and gave a careless wave of his hand.

Yet the thought of Judith lingered with him in a strange way, and he found himself seeking her company whenever he glimpsed her at Court. He didn't chance often upon her though. And she was always shy, but Tristram began to see that, whenever she talked, the things she said were level-headed, and at times uncommonly astute. Her manner was withdrawn, but there was something utterly compelling in the way she held herself and talked, something which, in his eyes, made her apart from all the other women he'd met so far. And she seemed restrained and gracious, and nothing at all like her gossipy Aunt Edith, who told him with an arched eyebrow in the Great Hall one day when they happened to meet, "My lord, I can see you've met my niece, Judith, the one who's promised to Raymond."

"Raymond?" Tristram asked striving to recall a lord knight called Raymond and failing.

"My stepson, Raymond," Lady Edith said, and Tristram now remembered who the lady was talking about.

"How old is the lad? Twelve?"

"Nearly thirteen," Lady Edith said tersely.

"And Lady Judith is how old?" Tristram couldn't help asking.

"Eighteen already since this winter," the lady replied. "Our own king was but a mere boy when he married our queen, who's more than ten years older, as you know," she added pointedly.

"Still, this boy is far too green for marriage," Tristram ventured, which earned him a dark look.

In the next days, he strove yet again to put the lady Judith away from his mind, because it was unseemly to think so ardently upon a woman who would one day pledge herself to another. He failed though.

It was with raised eyebrows that he listened, a week later, to what his mother had to say.

"Lord Edward of Redmore, Lady Judith's father," his mother told him upon their meal, "I have spoken to him."

"Why?" Tristram asked in sheer surprise.

"You're nearly four and twenty," his mother told him, as if the answer cleared everything for everyone.

"So?" Tristram shrugged, trying to look unruffled.

"Most of your friends have wed," his mother said pointedly. "I see no reason why you shouldn't think upon it."

"Well, I…"

"Sir Edward wishes to meet you. Our rank is higher than his at present, but he is of old blood, and some of his ancestors were Northumbrian princes. His lands are vast and he is wealthy."

"I have no wish to wed," Tristram countered hastily.

"Edward of Redmore's daughter has obviously taken your fancy. Is there any harm I already looked into this match for you? You could do even better, certainly, because you've both the rank and looks any woman would want. Yet, I know you. You're so like your late father!"

His mother trailed off with a wistful smile on her face.

"How so?" Tristram muttered already fearing the answer.

"Unlike most lords, your father thought marriage should be for love, and not for rank or wealth," his mother answered, and Tristram could still see the pain over his father's passing, fresh in her eyes, even after all these years.

"I do not lo–" he started, but his mother shushed him.

"Don't say it! Because perchance you will one day. Or even sooner than you think. And wouldn't that be a beautiful thing?"

He shook his head with a half-smile, understanding that, just like his father, his mother did believe in married love, so he resembled both his parents.

"Lady Edith has told me Judith of Redmore is already promised to another, so I hardly think it's proper of me to talk to her father," he started, but his mother shushed him again.

"That's not what Sir Edward told me," she countered.

IT WAS with disappointment mixed with a sort of relief that Judith received the summons to come to speak to her father in the lodgings they'd taken in London while Sir Edward had business at Court. This year was the first time Judith had come to Court, and it had been both bliss and torture to be here. She'd always wished to come here because she was fond of verse and song, and of the troubadours. However, Judith worried for her mother, who was so frail of health. Although she'd found true entertainment in this place, she couldn't help but think of her poor ailing mother, who, even after all these years, still pined for her sunny home in the South of France, and hadn't ever brought herself to like her English husband's Northern castle.

"Come, daughter," her father told her in his stern, gruff voice, beckoning her to come closer to where he stood.

Judith nodded, keeping her eyes downcast. Although he was her father, Judith knew him but little. She'd spent few moments in his company, as he'd been always busy. When she was little, she'd been afraid of even the sound of his voice, because her mother had always told her he was a harsh man. Yet she never recalled her father having ever laid a harsh hand upon her or ever having said something unkind. Still, she knew he was quite cruel and unfeeling to her mother. So she'd never been able to warm towards him.

Her father glanced at her awkwardly, as if not knowing what to say to her. He didn't speak a word of Occitan, and her mother had always refused to learn what she called the rough, coarse language of the serfs. Since her mother wouldn't speak English, her parents spoke Norman to each other, a language they both understood and spoke well, but which neither of them preferred. Perchance this was why they always spoke to each other so little.

"A match!" her father suddenly said in English and his voice sounded too loud to Judith's ears. "I've made a good match for you, daughter. You should be pleased!"

Judith raised her eyebrows, not understanding. She already knew of the match her mother wished to make for her. Her mother wanted her to wed Raymond, her sister Edith's stepson, and had assured her Raymond would one day grow up to be a fine husband for her. Judith had always been fond of her step-cousin just as she was of Lady Edith's true daughter, Emma. So she supposed that in six years from hence, she'd learn to love him as a wife should. Besides, it was sensible to wed someone one knew from childhood and not a stranger, so she tried to feel persuaded all would be well.

"Raymond, aye, Mother told me," she replied with a timid nod of her head.

Her father frowned darkly.

"Not Edith's pup! A man. A grown man of good birth and good breeding. A fine match indeed!"

Judith tried to still her thumping heart.

"A stranger?" she muttered, because, until this year, she'd never even visited London and had led her sheltered life at home, by her mother's side.

Judith enjoyed her sheltered life. It suited her quiet nature. She had her own songs and stories to keep her company and her beloved home, Redmore Castle, besides her mother whom she cherished. And the thought of wedding a stranger seemed simply terrifying to her.

"A fine man, you'll come to see," her father said, and his voice sounded gentler. "He wants to wed *you*."

Judith didn't like the stress her father placed upon the last of his words. It seemed he looked down upon what she was. And Judith knew herself not to be beautiful at all, or particularly clever. Her mother had not tried to hide these flaws from her, but had always told Judith she loved her dearly. Looks or great wit were not all that mattered in this world, her mother was fond to add.

Instead of seeing her look of sheer anguish, her father beamed at her. She'd seldom seen him happy. He usually looked sad and grim whenever he came to talk to her and her mother.

"You'll see, you'll be so pleased with this match, daughter," he said, glancing down upon her from his great height.

"A stranger…" Judith repeated, staring at him.

Her mother had warned her of this. She'd told Judith her father might wish to wed her to a stranger against her will, since he'd always been harsh and rather uncaring.

"But you're already acquainted," her father bellowed. "From Court. He's Tristram, Lord de Brunne!"

He looked mightily pleased when he uttered the name, and Judith bit hard into her lip. Now her father was making a cruel jest at her expense. Everyone knew Lord de Brunne was one of the most coveted men at Court. In Judith's eyes, he was simply beautiful, decidedly the most beautiful creature she'd ever had occasion to gaze upon. But looks weren't everything in this world, her mother had always wisely told her. So Judith had strived not to think too much upon Lord de Brunne. However, now it seemed her father had already perceived she fancied this lord, and he was making fun of her.

"You are to wed Tristram de Brunne in a fortnight hence," her father proclaimed, and by the way he uttered the words, Judith came to see in surprise that he was earnest.

She stared at him, simply stunned, and she found her voice only with difficulty.

"Wh-what if I do not wish to wed him?"

Her father frowned.

"Why wouldn't you wish to wed him?"

"Well…"

"Isn't he handsome and young?" her father asked.

"Yes. He is, but…"

"Isn't he well-born and wealthy?"

"Well-born, yes. Wealthy… I have not cared to ask…"

"I have," her father cut her off. "He's all of these things. He's also a sensible, honourable man, and the finest swordsman in the realm, and he wishes to marry *you*."

Again, Judith didn't like the way her father spoke the word.

"Perchance," she ventured. "But I do not wish to marry him."

"Why ever not?"

"Because… I do not care for him…"

Her father cast her a piercing look. It seemed he wanted to say something more, but then changed his mind and shook his head. At last he spoke, "In time you'll come to care for him. He is indeed a worthy man. And he has vowed to treat you right."

"He…" Judith searched her brain for things to say against Lord de Brunne and failed. This lord was not only handsome. He had a warm comely smile which always reached his fine dark eyes, and she'd never seen him treat a lady with disdain or unkindness. He was always courteous and most chivalrous to all. Tristram de Brunne was not only reputed to be the best swordsman in the realm. He was the best dancer she'd ever chanced upon and she supposed she'd never hear enough of his singing voice – the most melodious voice her ears had ever caught. In truth, when she'd first heard him speak, she'd thought her mind was playing tricks upon her. And Tristram de Brunne knew how to laugh and jest, and always said the cleverest and most diverting of things. Judith shook her head in sheer misery. She supposed she looked upon Tristram de Brunne with childish fancy, but she simply couldn't help herself. She'd never met a man who seemed so accomplished in every way. And she grimly told herself he was, certainly, a man too good to be true. He must have a hidden flaw or vice. Otherwise, how could such an accomplished man wish to marry somebody such as herself? Or was it just her father's wealth he craved?

"He…" Judith repeated stubbornly, searching for things to tell her father which would make him change his mind.

Her father seemed unconcerned. However, he attempted to place a hand upon her shoulder rather awkwardly. Judith found herself flinching from him, unused to her father ever touching her, and he withdrew his hand with a frown.

"All will be well, daughter. Have faith in me," he told her at last, and his voice sounded firm.

"But I do not wish to wed him," she countered in a weary voice which already sounded defeated to her own ears.

Why was she not trying harder to persuade her father she did not wish for this match?

"Yet you shall wed him as soon as can be, because he is the right match for you. And your scheming mother and that asp of a sister of hers can do nothing to stop this!" her father said in a decisive, self-satisfied voice.

A mere fortnight later Judith found herself staring upon the ring with carved initials which Lord de Brunne had slid upon her finger with a warm smile. Her half-hearted protests to her father had been to no avail, and Judith felt guilty for not bringing herself to stand up to him, knowing her mother would chide her for her cowardice. She simply hadn't had the strength to protest. She supposed she was a vain, shallow creature, enticed by the sheer beauty and charm of the man who sought to wed her. Otherwise, she'd have found the fortitude to resist the match. Judith now reasoned she was truly weak.

CHAPTER 4

*J*udith supposed she was weak and foolish to welcome the touch of a man set on humbling her. She'd not only let Tristram take her maidenhead last night, but she'd also shamelessly revelled in their lovemaking. And it was as if she'd unlocked the door of a forbidden chamber she could no longer close.

At present, Tristram, who plainly thought himself her master, was gazing upon her chastened behind. His fingers were boldly tracing the stripes his punishing belt had left upon her skin yesterday.

"So?" Judith asked, unable to contain her anguish. "Will you punish me now?"

Tristram's fingers were now no longer touching her reddened skin. When she gingerly sat up, he yawned as he stretched his hard body, and Judith, who'd never seen that beast which was called the leopard, but who'd seen painted images of it, supposed he now looked just like a leopard. It was perhaps not fitting that the De Brunne banner was an eagle soaring. It should have been a leopard *passant*.

Tristram didn't answer, and she found herself staring at him in vexation.

"Husband?" she queried.

"Not now. Later," he replied, beginning to comb his tousled fair hair with his fingers.

Judith had the urge of reaching out to do that for him, but stopped herself in time. She frowned to herself, because, while her bottom felt much better than she'd thought it would, it still smarted when she sat down on it.

"Later," she muttered with a sigh. "Later… when?"

He shrugged, unconcernedly, and Judith knew he was doing so because he wanted to taunt her. Judith had already become resigned she would have to submit to her husband's punishments. However, she didn't see why she should submit to his taunts.

"I'd rather you did it now, to get it done and over with," she said, although the moment she spoke the words she realized she'd given Tristram the perfect excuse to torment her.

"I bet you would," Tristram grinned in full malice.

The next thing he did though took her by surprise, and she didn't even have the time to catch her breath as, lightning-fast, she found herself lying face down over his lap.

"You are defiant, wife," Tristram chided, as he began to rub her bottom. "And to cure you of your defiance, methinks I'll punish you both now and later."

"What?"

But Judith didn't have the time to say anything further, as Tristram's large hand came swiftly to spank her bottom. The spank he delivered wasn't hard, but Judith instantly gasped in surprise under it. Her bottom was still quite tender from yesterday. And she began to understand how foolish she'd been to goad her lord to spank her now. He would reduce her to tears in a matter of moments. And Judith understood, with a thumping heart, he may want to use the same belt he'd used yesterday. She bit her lip, hard, coming to see she'd not thought this through.

"Husband, I…"

Tristram's hand now caught her sit spots, which caused a mightier burn than before and a treacherous, ignoble stir in her sex. She attempted to feel ashamed of it, and failed.

"My lord…"

The punishing hand had blissfully stopped, and Judith felt disgusted with how grateful she now was that he'd desisted.

"You were saying, wife?" he asked in a silky voice.

"I…"

Judith hated herself for what she would say next, but there was no going around this.

"I erred. It's best you spank me later," she muttered, now simply revelling in the warm weight of his large, rough hand upon her behind.

Smack. Suddenly, Tristram's hand was no longer still, as he delivered a volley of rapid spanks on her very tender behind, which instantly brought tears to her eyes. Mercifully though, he let her off without continuing what he'd started, and yet again Judith hated herself for the strange, unseemly feelings which rose inside her. This was punishment, but in her feverish mind this ignoble chastisement had already turned into strange love play.

She sniffed, rubbing her bottom in an undignified manner, while Tristram perused her with his dark eyes. There was undisguised heat she read there, and she simply blushed, lowering her gaze.

"Tonight I'll finish what I started," he let her know and his voice sounded hard, quite at odds with the liquid warmth in his eyes.

She nodded, dejected, thinking upon the very different way he'd treated her when they'd first wed. At first she'd thought him the most wondrous, kindest man who had ever lived. But then her mother had made her see what he was in truth. Or so she'd thought. Because at this moment she was older and different than she'd been. And she had come to see her mother hadn't been right at all times. Still, she recalled what she'd seen with her own eyes, and anger came back in full blazes. Tristram now meant to punish her fiercely for lying to him. But who would ever punish him for lying to her as he had during their marriage?

As soon as she was dressed, she went to see her mother, trying to look calm and unconcerned, so Lady Fenice wouldn't worry unduly. Judith already feared yesterday's events had made her mother's mind even more frenzied and melancholy than it had been of late.

"He's plucked you," her mother said abruptly, casting her a sad, appraising look, just as soon as Judith entered the solar where Lady Fenice spent all her time.

Judith placed the tray she'd been carrying on the table by her mother's side, saying nothing.

"I saw it from my window, how he dragged you after him in the inner bailey. I couldn't see what happened next. Did he beat you?"

Judith shrugged, replaying the punishment she'd received at her husband's hands. It had been a harsh spanking, yet she had to be honest to herself. It hadn't been a beating. She opened her mouth to tell her mother that, apart from a sore bottom, she was unharmed, but her mother didn't let her speak.

"My poor daughter!" she muttered with a chagrined expression on her face.

"You needn't worry..." Judith started, but yet again, her mother didn't let her finish.

"He beat you and then he ravished you. So like a man!"

"He didn't ravish me!"

"Oh."

For a moment, to Judith it seemed her mother's voice was disappointed, but she decided her mind was playing tricks on her.

"Of course," her mother said with a mocking smile. "I had forgotten. He is a clever fiend, that one. He's finally tricked you into lying with him."

Judith took a deep breath, telling herself it was only of late her mother had become so distraught and troubled. Or… The nagging thought which hadn't let her be for many months came back to haunt her. Or was it that her mother had always been distraught and troubled, and Judith was only now beginning to grasp it? How could it be? Judith decided, whatever the truth, her mother loved her dearly and had always wished the best for her. She always worried over her daughter, as she should.

"We should escape as soon as can be, you and I," her mother went on, and it seemed she wasn't talking to Judith, but to herself. "To go to my sister. And then who knows, perchance I'll get to see my beloved home in Aquitaine before I die."

"Aunt Edith cannot aid us now. She's supported Eleanor, just as we did, and Eleanor is vanquished. She will probably have to go into exile. And, Mother, you have not left these chambers in several years, not even to walk through the bailey. How will you be able to undertake such a long journey?"

Her mother sighed.

"I have been ailing. I will get stronger though, and we will be able to leave this accursed place!"

Judith said nothing at first. For many years she'd thought her mother was suffering in her body. But in the last year she had come to finally understand it was not her mother's body that was ailing. A year ago, Judith had prevailed upon her mother to have one of the greatest physicians in the land call upon her – a man reputed to have studied the art of healing in the Holy Land. And the healer had told the truth of it to Judith. There was no affliction of the body which plagued the lady Fenice. She was just heart-broken and forlorn.

"I do not think this place is accursed," she decided to tell her mother gently, as she was pouring her a goblet of watered wine. "It has always been my home. And you've not received news of your kin there in many years. Besides, our people are here and we have a duty to them."

Her mother scoffed.

"Not my people. Just Englishmen."

"I call myself an Englishwoman," Judith countered in the same gentle voice as she'd employed before.

She had already expected her mother wouldn't understand, but she hoped the lady Fenice would become reconciled with the way things were. Tristram might hate Judith now and might want to exact his revenge upon her, but he had his own honour, and he would never harm or mistreat her mother. Lady Fenice would be safe here – safer and happier than in a convent. As for Aquitaine, Judith doubted her mother would indeed ever be able to make the journey, no matter how hard she wished for it.

Her mother's harsh laughter took her by surprise. Lady Fenice had always been gentle and soft-spoken, and it seemed strange that today she was behaving so unlike herself. But Judith decided the castle's surrender had increased her mother's distress.

"It's clear you have no wish to get away. My poor daughter, you lust for the fiend! I always knew it," her mother said with that peculiar, harsh laughter.

Lust was not a word Judith ever recalled her mother to have used. She blushed, lowering her eyes. Nevertheless Lady Fenice was right. Her mother knew her well. Judith attempted to conjure up guilt for her own weakness, and she recalled, with flushed cheeks, the brazen, heated coupling she and Tristram had shared last night. She should feel guilty for her ignoble enjoyment of all of it, and even guiltier for the shameful way she'd felt this morning as she'd lain defenceless across her husband's lap. Yet she simply found she couldn't feel guilty.

"All will be well, Mother. We've not been driven from our home," she said, now belatedly recalling the letter she'd once received from the bishop's chancery which had stated her marriage to Tristram had been annulled.

In the turmoil of events which had unfolded, she'd not had the time to think upon it. But now as she was able to do so, she shook her head in sheer puzzlement. How could a chancery clerk have erred so grievously?

She recalled the day she'd received the letter, and how she'd told herself she should be happy her marriage to a man who didn't and couldn't ever care for her was done and over with. And how she'd strived to put Tristram away from her mind. She'd failed though – miserably. His face and voice had forever haunted her dreams. And now they were together again. Judith attempted to tell herself she should look upon this only with bitterness. Yet it was not only bitterness she conjured up whenever she thought of Tristram.

CHAPTER 5

*T*ristram's temples were pounding hard this morning, although, in truth, he'd drunk no more than half a cup of wine last night. It seemed though as if he was recovering from a heavy bout of drinking. He swore under his breath. Certainly, he'd been drunk on his wife's charms, although he'd promised himself to be distant and cold. His friend, Bertran FitzRolf cast him a searching glance as they were lightly sparring with staves, as was their usual practice in the morning.

"All's well?" FitzRolf asked, and Tristram contented himself to shrug as he glimpsed his cousin approaching them with a pinched look on his gaunt face. Isidore didn't bid them a good morrow.

"I saw your wife walking about this morn, guiding the servants and seeing to her people. I told her to wear a modest headdress!" he called out with a scowl.

Tristram raised his eyebrows, setting his staff aside. Judith had covered her hair as of this morning, as was required of all married women. So why was Isidore scoffing?

"That thing! That vile thing they call a *barbette*!" Isidore ranted. "Just as that lewd Eleanor used to wear at Court. That's not headcover! It's a disgrace!"

Judith had now indeed covered her hair, but like most noble married women of Tristram's acquaintance, it was not her habit to wear a heavy wimple which covered her neck and hid all her glorious hair. Tristram recalled that in the first days of their marriage she'd worn a filet and a dainty embroidered veil, and upon this morning she'd had upon her that item they called a *barbette*, which Queen Eleanor had brought with her from the South of France. It had a band under the chin, but was designed in such a way as to leave part of the crown of a woman's hair uncovered. Tristram recalled prelates had chided the Queen over this, but many women at Court had adopted the fashion. He did not particularly care for this item, or for any kind of headdress, because he loved to see Judith's black hair uncovered. Nevertheless it was not what custom decreed, and Isidore was here, watching like a hawk over them.

"My lady has indeed covered her hair, just as you asked, hasn't she?" Tristram said, attempting to sound unconcerned.

A younger son, destined from infancy for the Church, Tristram's cousin Isidore spent most of his time in prayer and fasting, and mortifying his flesh. Isidore de Brunne was thought a pious man, even more pious than Thomas Becket, people whispered. And Henry seemed to hold him in as much esteem as he'd held Becket once. Unlike Becket however, Isidore was no commoner. Their family was of high birth. And Tristram knew his cousin would use that to his advantage and secure a high rank for himself in the Church.

"Your woman does not look at all humbled, though you vowed to make her repent," his cousin said pointedly, and Tristram stifled a sigh.

"She is my wife, and I mean to see to her chastisement," he countered, casting a hard stare at Isidore whose scowl deepened.

"You made a vow. It seems though she has you ensorcelled. A

haughty woman, this wife of yours. Although I recall you once claimed her ways were mild and shy."

"I've already chastened her this morning. And I plan to chasten her again, just as I vowed. And you shall soon see she will learn true repentance for her deeds," Tristram said wearily.

"Aye, repentance not only for her defiance of her liege lord and of her lord husband, but also for the insult she's brought upon our noble house!"

Tristram's cousin still chafed upon the way in which Judith had sought to annul her marriage to a De Brunne, and thought it his duty to avenge their family's honour.

"I've punished her and will not tarry to do so again. I am upholding my oath. What more do you want of me?" Tristram called out sharply.

His cousin shook his head in full bitterness.

"I see only too well the way you look at her. She already has you twisted around her little finger. Do you think me blind? And she deserves far more punishment for what she did. *True* punishment! You know it as well as I."

"She has been punished. And she'll be further punished, never fear," Tristram countered.

"Or so you say," his cousin retorted drily, before heading to the chapel for his long prayers of the morning.

Tristram felt thankful at least that his cousin had not attempted to replace the castle's chaplain for the time he was residing at Redmore. Father Thomas was, as he recalled from his earlier days at Redmore, a kindly man and far less austere than his cousin. Tristram hoped Isidore would not seek to oversee the spiritual welfare of Redmore in Father Thomas' stead. He wished to avoid that at all costs.

"He has a cruel streak in him, your cousin, like many church-men," FitzRolf muttered with a shake of his head, as they watched upon Isidore's gaunt form heading towards the chapel.

Tristram nodded with a frown. If it had been entirely up to

his cousin and the Church, Judith was to have received a flogging and had her hair shorn as a mark of her shame. And if it had been entirely up to the Church and to his family, Tristram was supposed to have sent his wife to spend the rest of her life locked in a convent. Yet Henry truly ruled over the Church in this land, ever since Thomas Becket had been killed, and Tristram had pleaded with Henry. He'd taken it upon himself to formally bestow a punishment on his miscreant wife. A punishment harsh enough to satisfy those called to witness it. And he supposed he'd failed in that task. Isidore was to report to Henry and to the Church, and Isidore wasn't happy, thinking the discipline Tristram had bestowed upon his lady had been too mild.

"You did what you could. I do not think I could have done any better in your stead," FitzRolf said with a sigh, obviously guessing Tristram's thoughts.

Tristram conjured up the punishment he'd delivered. It had been good he was angry with Judith. His anger had helped him harden his heart against her when he'd used the belt. Even in his anger, he'd not been able to bring himself to give her anything other than a good spanking. Isidore had wanted a harsh beating. And *that* Tristram had been unable to provide.

"I hope we'll soon see the back of him," Tristram muttered grimly, knowing, however, his overly zealous, austere cousin would not be so easy to dismiss.

His cousin took his ecclesiastical duties far too seriously, just as Thomas Becket had. Tristram supposed it was blasphemous of him to think it, but he fully agreed with King Henry that Becket's extreme fervour had been a menace to their land.

"When he is finally persuaded you're able to keep your wife subdued and well chastened, I suppose he will at last go back to London. And I with him," FitzRolf said rather wistfully.

Tristram cast his friend a sympathetic look. It had been many months since Bertran FitzRolf had glanced upon his own wife, and FitzRolf loved that wife of his quite dearly. Tristram couldn't help but picture a world where he himself had a wife he loved dearly, and who loved him dearly in return. It was what he had wished for when he'd wed Judith. Yet things hadn't turned out to be the way he'd wished them. And now, due to the course of the war which had torn their country, both Judith and he had to suffer each other for the rest of their lives. Still… he recalled the lust they'd shared and the heated abandon with which his wife had given herself to him. It was strange. Now he'd decided he would have no love between them, and that he would be harsh to her rather than gentle, things seemed to have settled far more easily. Perhaps he had been wrong those years ago, and there was no true place for love or gentleness in this marriage. Lust and heat and harshness were perchance the only way in which he could deal with his wife.

"How fares the lady Judith?" FitzRolf asked, astute as always when his friend's thoughts were concerned.

"Her bottom's still sore, but other than that she fares quite well," Tristram muttered, unable to shed from his mind the plans of heated discipline he had in store for his wife.

"She's different than you described her to me," FitzRolf suddenly said, and this made Tristram frown.

"How so?" he queried.

"The woman you talked to me about was shy and withdrawn and skittish. Uncertain of herself at times. But it is not how I perceived your wife. She seems self-assured and more than capable in caring for her people. And she bore the surrender of her home and the punishment far better than I thought she would."

When his friend went to oversee their men's training, Tristram had occasion to muse upon what had been said. Perhaps Bertran had the right of it. Tristram himself had noticed a change in Judith. She was far bolder and more decisive than she'd been years ago. And the passionate manner in which she'd responded to his lovemaking had nothing to do with the timid maiden she'd been when they'd first wed. But perhaps this was no change at all. Judith herself had told him last night she had been lying to him. The way she'd acted then had surely been part of her treachery and deceit. But why had Judith wanted to wreck their marriage? It was a question he'd often thought upon during the time they'd been apart. And there was no clear answer he could conjure up. He'd treated his lady graciously and had sought to earn her love. And for a while he'd thought she could easily grow to love him. But then she'd spurned and betrayed him.

He raked a hand through his hair, knowing that what he'd resolved upon could not be undone. More than a year ago Henry had prevailed upon the Church not to grant the annulment of Tristram's marriage. Redmore was one of the few stone castles in England, and Henry would have only someone loyal to him oversee it. The king had known too well that while Judith's father had been alive, he'd had Redmore's allegiance. After Sir Edward's passing, it had however become plain Judith and her Occitan mother were loyal to Queen Eleanor's cause. And Henry was shrewd enough not to sever the bond between the heir of Redmore and a De Brunne. The De Brunnes had always been loyal to their king. So it was convenient for Henry that the De Brunnes should keep their ties to Redmore.

Tristram's marriage to Judith had been convenient for Henry as long as Eleanor was still a threat. Now Eleanor lay vanquished, and Judith was no longer a valuable pawn in Henry's game. When it had become clear Redmore could be easily taken, the King had advised Tristram to cast Judith aside as soon as the castle was captured. The Church and Tristram's family had urged that the miscreant wife be harshly chastised, and then forced to take the veil. But Tristram had not wanted it so. He'd sought to be magnanimous to Judith even if she'd betrayed him, and had meant to let her seek her sanctum in the South of France with her lady mother. He had not truly expected her to comply with his haughty terms of letting her stay on at Redmore as his wife, because he'd come to understand she despised him. Nevertheless, he should have guessed Judith would, after all, want to stay, in spite of her disgust with him. She loved her home and her people far too much to go.

Tristram heaved a deep sigh. He'd made an oath to chastise his wife for her misdeeds and have her repent, because they'd all demanded it of him. Henry, his family, the Church… As long as he decided not to cast her away, he was forever bound to ensure her obedience. Last night he hadn't meant to claim Judith. He still resented her, and he supposed it had been petty of him to want to taunt her for what she'd done to him. He'd meant to humiliate her just as she'd humiliated him, expecting she would never be able to bring herself to touch him. Yet Judith had touched him. She had done much more than touch him. And then he'd found himself unable to rein in his lust for her. Now it was done. She was in truth his wife. *His wife* – the wife he still lusted after and who, as it turned out, lusted after him in spite of herself. Tristram smiled bitterly. Lust for her he may, but he no longer sought to love her – *he never would*. A loveless marriage – he'd doomed himself to it by allowing Judith to stay, and there was no undoing it now.

∽

FOUR YEARS AGO, 1170

THE BEDDING CEREMONY was an ordeal to Judith, because she'd always been shy, and now she had to display her naked body in front of her new husband and strangers. She and Tristram were forced to stand naked facing each other, in order for the wedding attendants to confirm both the bride and groom were hale and fit for marriage. At last, the door closed behind the last of the wedding attendants, and Judith tried to avert her eyes from Tristram's beautiful form, knowing she found even his manhood beautiful. It now stood unashamedly erect in front of her. She tried to tell herself she should be very afraid of it, just as her aunt Edith had cautioned her, when she'd readied her for the bedding.

"Men of Sir Tristram's ilk have their urges. It will hurt mightily when his rod tears through your maidenhead," her aunt Edith had told her with a sad shake of her head as she was combing Judith's long luscious hair, in preparation for her wedding night.

Judith had said nothing, recalling her mother had also told her most men had brutish urges, which were a trial to their God-fearing wives. Yet Tristram de Brunne had always been gracious to her, and she had a hard time reconciling the fluid, elegant manner in which he always carried himself with the savage ways of a brutish beast.

"You'll have to suffer him, because this is Eve's lot. Have a care though not to succumb to his sinful ways," Aunt Edith had cautioned her, handling the brush somewhat forcefully on Judith's mass of midnight dark hair, which made Judith wince.

"Sinful ways..." Judith had muttered, not fully understanding.

She'd often heard priests speak of the sins of the flesh, but she'd mostly turned a deaf ear on what they had to say, because the ways of the flesh hadn't been her concern at all. But now she would be a married woman.

"You will know what they are, because they're plainly sinful!" her aunt Edith had scoffed, but hadn't enlightened her in any way.

Sinful? Judith now mused, trying to hide her blush. Would Tristram kissing her ardently count as sinful? Would Tristram's long-fingered hands caressing her naked breasts count as sinful? Would her brushing her lips against those impossibly thick dark lashes of his beautiful eyes count as sinful? Would... There were so many things she pictured in her mind she could share with Tristram.

And now, as the wedding attendants had blissfully left, she was alone with Tristram, and they were both naked. She blushed fiercely, knowing full well he was utterly beautiful and she was only plain, and he must have certainly already perceived that. Frantically, she searched for the shift her attendants had removed during the bedding ceremony. She spotted it at last. It had been discarded on the floor, and now it lay at Tristram's feet. And Tristram simply bent to pick it up and handed it wordlessly to her. Judith hastily slipped into it, knowing he needn't have her fully naked in order to do the deed he had to do tonight. And perhaps Tristram didn't care to see her naked. He'd been, she was certain, already used to bedding women who must have been far more comely than she was.

Tristram picked up his own discarded fur-lined robe and put it on, which caused her to suppress a sigh of sheer regret.

"Some wine, my lady?" he asked courteously, going to fetch the pitcher and goblets the wedding attendants had brought for them.

Judith nodded in some relief. She didn't know what to do with herself, so drinking wine would keep her busy for a while.

"Perchance our wedding was too sudden," Tristram said abruptly as he took a sip from his own goblet of wine. "I wished for a long betrothal, but your father prevailed upon me for an early wedding, telling me you were not adverse to it."

Judith widened her eyes. She'd had a chance to glance upon Tristram in the two weeks which had led to the wedding. But during those occasions she'd had the opportunity to be with him, she'd been hardly able to open her mouth, because his presence nearly always reduced her to a loss of words. Judith was shy, but she'd never been this tongue-tied. Whenever Tristram had spoken to her, she'd nodded eagerly to whatever he'd been saying, unable to refrain from staring at him with wide eyes and a tremulous smile, which must have made her look like a lovesick simpleton. Was it love, this childish fancy she felt whenever she glanced upon Tristram de Brunne? Was it plain, sinful lust? Both at the same time?

Tristram sighed.

"It all has been too hasty, hasn't it? You see, I…"

He paused, as if at a loss for words, which was strange, because she'd never known Tristram de Brunne to lack for words. He was the best-spoken lord she'd ever met, and one of those men who never talked down to women. She'd been aware of that as soon as she'd met him. Unlike her father or other lords and knights of her acquaintance, it seemed he had the patience to listen closely whenever women spoke. It was a rare virtue for a man to have.

Tristram suddenly smiled.

"Yet you so eagerly said *aye* when I asked you plainly if you would have me!"

Judith frowned, striving to recall him ever having asked the question, and simply failing. It must have been that first day when he'd come to call upon her after her father had told her of his plans. She'd been in such turmoil that she'd been able to focus just on the music of his voice as he'd spoken, eagerly agreeing from time to time to whatever he had to say. She had been loath to betray she was unable to even make sense of what he'd been saying. He'd tried to coax her to talk to him, but all she'd managed had been acquiescent responses to all his attempts to engage her in conversation.

Tristram must have noted the dismay in her eyes, because he hurried to say, "Nevertheless, things have been far too hasty. And you need more time to get accustomed to me. Rest assured, my lady, I will not press upon you to surrender your maidenhead tonight. We'll take things slowly. There's time enough to learn each other's ways and bodies."

Judith felt deep relief mixed with strange disappointment.

Yet it was best this way. Her new lord had given her a reprieve, and that was certainly gracious of him.

"Aye, husband," she muttered dumbly, as always not knowing what to say in his presence.

"I like the way the word *husband* sounds upon your lips," he told her, and his warm smile reached his sinfully dark eyes, as he gently took her hand in his.

Judith's heart started thumping wildly. Why was it that it was to this very man, the only one who made her heart race like mad, that she'd gotten married? He unsettled her far too much.

"And will you now call me by my name?" Tristram asked in that voice of his which had sweet music in it.

"What? Tristram?" she whispered.

"Mm," he acquiesced, as his hand slowly began to caress her palm and fingers.

Judith had never known that such a simple, seemingly innocent caress could feel so hot, and she bit her lip in sheer surprise. And Tristram mistook her surprise for shock, because he swiftly withdrew his hand.

"Let us just talk tonight," he said with a soothing smile. "I like to hear your voice."

As always, Judith had agreed to what he said, and they had started talking. He'd asked her more of her home and had told her of his in exchange, and Judith had gradually begun to feel less tongue-tied in his presence. And she'd told him of Redmore, and of how much she cared for her home and for her people and for the hills and moorland she loved to roam, coming to understand Tristram was indeed one of those rare men who knew how to listen, not only how to talk.

CHAPTER 6

*I*n her bedchamber, Judith stirred from her memories at the sound of Tristram's voice. Tristram's voice, which had always been gentle and soft in her memories, was now simply hard and flinty. A beautiful voice still, even in its flintiness.

"Come here, wife," Tristram said patting his lap, and there was no doubt in Judith's mind concerning what he meant to do.

She heaved a heartfelt sigh, but obeyed his command, because it was true she now lived on his sufferance.

He hoisted her skirts to look upon her and Judith blushed scarlet as he did so. She knew her bottom was still striped with pink, but as evening had neared, it had begun to smart less fiercely than it had this morning after his ministrations. She sighed again, fully knowing that this blissful state wouldn't last long because her now stern husband meant to chastise her, just as he'd promised.

"Still sore, wife?" he asked in a soft voice, as he was sliding his calloused palm over the skin of her bare bottom and thighs.

"Why are you asking me this? Do you care?" she countered, knowing whatever she uttered, he would still spank her.

He laughed cruelly, saying, as if he'd guessed her very thoughts, "To be sure, for these words, I'll spank you even harder."

Judith gnashed her teeth, to prevent the retort which sprang on her tongue.

"What? No further words of defiance?" Tristram asked, brushing his fingers tantalizingly over her buttocks.

Judith supposed what she did next would not lighten her punishment, but she just couldn't help herself. She cursed, foully, because Tristram's fingers kindled a shameful, powerful sensation inside her quim, even if he'd not even touched her there.

"Ah," Tristram said in full, grim satisfaction, and he proceeded to spank her soundly with his hand, soon putting a fire in her behind which first matched, and then even surpassed the one she'd felt this morning.

The spanking left her weak-kneed and crying, but that powerful, shameful feeling inside her quim became even more maddening. When Tristram finally let her off his lap, Judith rubbed her bottom frantically, although, in truth, it was not only her bottom she wanted to rub. She desperately wanted to touch herself between her legs, to ease the shameful, powerful fire her husband's spanking had kindled there.

As before, Tristram sat watching her with avid dark eyes which looked both hard and warm.

"Be thankful I spared you the belt," he said lazily.

Judith couldn't help but glare at him, feeling the insane urge of both strangling him and of begging him to thrust inside her and give her release.

Tristram cocked a dark eyebrow.

"Yet I see you're not thankful for it."

His eyes seemed to be searching around the room, and Judith prayed fervently he wasn't looking for that accursed belt.

"I-I'm thankful for it, husband," she muttered reluctantly, through gritted teeth.

"Oh, are you?" Tristram asked making his voice a silky caress, and Judith knew she could no longer keep the rein of her temper.

"You love this – tormenting me!" she spat.

"Yes," Tristram said tersely, but Judith now perceived the odd, strained note in his voice she had heard before when he'd confirmed he'd kept her on for revenge.

It was however with relief that she saw he hadn't fetched the belt. Instead he ordered her to lie on her elbows and knees in their bed, and he knelt behind her. Judith began to wonder frantically if he had more punishment in store for her, but she gasped in sheer mortification as she swiftly understood he'd bent his head to unashamedly lick her sex in that undignified position, with her bottom thrust towards him.

"So very wet already – gushing," he muttered, and his voice no longer sounded hard, but warm, just like the voice of the Tristram whom she recalled from their first days of marriage.

Judith simply moaned when his tongue thrust inside her. It was a humiliating position and what he was doing was certainly sinful. Yet Judith decided she'd already received chastisement for her sins. And soon her husband's sinful tongue began to lick not only her quim, but also her poor chastened bottom. She'd nearly already climaxed with the sheer pleasure of what he'd done, when he finally deigned to grab her hips and rub his engorged cock against her bottom and sex.

"I should have spanked you on our wedding night, wife," he said softly, when she thought she would start begging him to claim her. "It would not only have taught you to mind me, it would have made your quim gush for me. Just as it's gushing now."

So he'd already perceived her shameful, twisted enjoyment of what he'd done. Judith's cheeks began to burn even more deeply, but soon she had occasion to focus on a different kind of fire. She nearly climaxed as soon as he plunged swiftly inside her from behind. He thrust hard, going in and out of her, as his front was making slapping contact with her freshly spanked rear. A fierce pleasure in her sex, and a fierce burn in her bottom. Judith soon forgot herself entirely, and she forgot to feel ashamed. She climaxed, but he didn't seem to care, still thrusting inside her with a vengeance, and, after a while, Judith's body melted again into a frenzy of pleasure, just as he shouted his own release, spilling his hot seed inside her.

They both collapsed, spent, but Judith could only lie on her belly, because her spanked bottom still tingled fiercely.

"I know now how I erred when we were newly married. I should have treated you harshly from the start. I was too gentle," Tristram said in a savage voice.

And suddenly Judith had the urge to weep at his words. She breathed in deep, trying to contain her anguish.

"What? Is there nothing you wish to tell me now, wife?" he tossed, as he was wiping his cock with the bed sheet.

"What is it that you wish me to tell you?" Judith asked wearily, as she rose to clean herself.

She supposed he would spank her anew for her defiance, but she was too spent and now past caring. What had gone on had shaken her too deeply. And his words – the bitterness with which he'd spoken them... They hadn't sounded like the words of a man set on cold revenge for his hurt pride. They'd sounded like the words of a man who'd been deeply hurt. But how could this be? Tristram had never had genuine regard for her. She had been just his plaything.

"I wish..." Tristram's voice was just an angry whisper, and he suddenly fell silent.

Judith felt too spent and weary to ask him what he'd meant.

When she came back to bed she just lay on her belly, in sheer exhaustion, not caring if her husband might have further punishment in store for her. Hazily, when she was dozing off, she felt a blanket coming to cover her, and, in the nearing slumber, she nearly smiled as she spoke the name of the man she'd in truth, never stopped loving madly, not even when she'd tried to deceive herself.

"Tristram," she whispered just before she was fast asleep.

CHAPTER 7

*T*ristram frowned upon hearing Judith's lovely voice call his name, knowing full well it was the first time she'd spoken it since he'd stormed into her castle. And he strived to harden his heart against her, because she'd brought him nothing but anguish and grief, and she didn't care for him. Yet he failed. Because he recalled those nights they'd shared in the first days of their marriage, when there'd been no heated caresses between them but only talk. And he recalled he'd loved talking to her, not only because he would never have enough of hearing her voice, but because, once she'd let go of her shyness, Judith had shown him she really had a way with words.

FOUR YEARS AGO, 1170

Tristram had refrained from touching his wife in those first nights they'd spent together, because he'd thought to give her time to get accustomed to him, without pressing. He had also discovered he enjoyed the tantalizing feeling of having her within reach without being able to touch her. It was courtship. And he had become aware they perhaps both needed to enjoy this chaste courtship until they moved on to heated caresses. They had plenty of time, and a life ahead together. Once Judith became more at ease in his presence, he reasoned she would ask for his ardent touch herself, and there really was nothing to be gained by rushing things unduly.

"Why is it you never speak English to me?" he asked her lazily one night, as they were lying chastely in their bed together. "In truth, I'm more accustomed to speaking English than Norman, and I know you are not Norman, but Occitan from your mother's side, just like our queen. However, your father is English."

Judith had laughed, that rich, melodious laughter he'd come to love.

"Fine. I shall speak English to you then," she said, and her voice was teasing.

Then she did speak to him in a language he barely recognized. It certainly sounded like English, but he was able to understand only some words of it.

"What kind of English is this?" he muttered in puzzlement.

"My English," she said in a voice full of laughter. "The English of the North. It's different from yours. Didn't you know?"

Tristram had never travelled North, but he recalled people said Northerners' speech was rough and different from that of the South or Midlands. To him, Judith's English didn't sound rough at all though, but strangely musical in its own way.

"Oh, just keep talking! I have a keen ear and I think I'll soon be able to follow more of what you say," he urged, smiling in the dark.

"Oh really? Would you be able to follow a story in verse if I tell you one?" Judith asked in Norman, but then reverted to Northern English to tell him the tale of the owl and the nightingale.

Tristram could not follow everything she was saying. He nevertheless soon became absorbed in the versed tale, where a grim owl perched on a bough argued with a vain nightingale. Some words of it sounded strange and he had trouble keeping up with the rhythm of her speech, but he made himself listen closely. He'd never heard the tale before, but he soon came to understand that most of its intricate verses were due to Judith's own cleverness. Judith may be shy, but now she was quite at ease in his company and she could revel in her passion for words. He found himself loving her English verse just as much as he loved her Occitan songs, even if it was still somewhat hard for him to follow what she was saying.

"So who did you like best, the owl or the nightingale?" Judith asked in Norman with a smile in her voice when she was done with her tale.

"I liked best the wren which comes to make peace between these two birds," Tristram countered with a smile of his own.

"The wren is wise," Judith conceded. "Yet whom would you choose as the victor of the debate, the useful owl or the beautiful nightingale?"

"Is there a choice? Both have their uses!" Tristram retorted, knowing Judith was not really asking him a question, but only liked to engage him in a debate not unlike the one in the tale she'd just told him.

She was quite clever, he'd come to see, even cleverer than he'd thought at first, but modest about her own wit and very seldom displaying it in front of others. And her gift for words far surpassed his own. She was already a troubadour, able to weave songs more wondrous than Queen Eleanor's most lauded poets. He'd once attempted to tell her she should bring her lute to Court and entertain more people with her songs, yet she was still shy in other people's presence, and Tristram had not pressed. For now Judith seemed happy not to share her songs with many people, and he had come to understand that making them was far more valuable to her than sharing them with others. It was wondrous and strange that a woman so quiet in other people's presence had such a way with words when there was just the two of them. And he felt the most fortunate of men, this woman was now his wife.

Soon they began to play a game of rhymes in Norman, and in this language Tristram could hold his own against Judith, although he had to admit she was still better than him at it. When they were done, he thought of bestowing a kiss upon her lips, but he felt strangely shy himself of it. Was it as his mother had told him? That he was already coming to love Judith? Or was it that he'd indeed fallen in love with her just the first time he'd chanced to hear her mermaid-like voice?

"Tell me of Redmore," he soon urged her, because he would never have enough of hearing her warm voice, and she loved best to talk of her childhood home.

Soon Judith's compelling voice began to tell him of Redmore.

"Some people may find it stark, and the warmth of the South is not to be found there. The hills are green in spring, but russet in autumn. The cliffs are further ahead and they are treacherous at times. It's often windy, but this is how I like it – the wind ruffling my hair when it's unbound. And in summer, the heather moorland is a wonder to behold – all purple, but there's dark blue bilberries mingling within. I do not think such colours are to be found in many places in this world, although to Mother they seem dreary – she misses her warm home in Aquitaine, where colours are bright and the sky is always azure."

Tristram had already learnt Judith was very fond of her mother, and she worried over the lady's frail health. And soon Judith would go back home to see to the ailing Lady Fenice. Tristram thought upon this with regret because he would have loved to keep his new bride by his side in London, yet he understood she was impatient to know her mother was well. He hadn't had the heart to tell her nay when she'd told him she needed to go back to Redmore so soon after their marriage. They'd spent but two brief weeks together, and Tristram supposed it would have been better to already share their bodies as they would be parted for some months.

He fell asleep with a suppressed sigh and a smile, telling himself it would be best to let Judith bring herself to ask for his caress. He had come to see she got tense and flustered whenever he attempted to touch her more ardently. And he resolved she might have let go of her shyness in their talk, but that she still needed to lose her maidenly fear of being touched by him. No matter, he told himself before drifting into sleep. He could see only too well Judith was already coming to care for him and soon her fear would melt. Once she was back from Redmore they would become husband and wife in truth.

CHAPTER 8

*J*udith left her new husband with regret in her heart, knowing a part of her would have liked nothing better than to have him hold her in his arms and make her his true wife. She however resolved he was right in not pressing her and in prolonging their courtship. There was another part of her which was shy and skittish, yet not of him, but rather because she was afraid she would show him from the start how utterly besotted and at his mercy she really was. She fancied this beautiful man far too much, and perchance he would not like her behaving like a lovesick fool, but as a restrained, dignified wife. So perchance it was wiser to prolong their courtship, just as Tristram wanted.

When Judith came to Redmore to look upon her mother, Lady Fenice looked pale and forlorn, although she tried to smile brightly as she cast her eyes upon her daughter. Yet Judith saw at once that something was amiss.

"Oh Mother, I missed you so!" she said, kissing her mother's cheek.

She suddenly felt guilty for the joyous news she wished to share with her mother. And she felt guilty that Sir Edward had decided upon this match without having the courtesy to ask for his wife's advice. Judith had tried to speak to her father upon this, but he had been set in arranging a hasty marriage for her, proclaiming he knew what was best for his daughter. Suddenly, Judith's genuine happiness over her match seemed out of place in her mother's chambers. Yet, as always, her mother soon inquired after her, and Judith found herself speaking of her new husband, or at least attempting to do so.

"My lord Tristram… He is…"

Judith stopped herself with a short, strained laugh. She'd meant to say Lord Tristram de Brunne was simply wondrous, but now, seeing her mother's keen eyes upon her, she came to understand the word was childish and silly.

"He is a good, worthy man," she said instead. "And I can see he means to be a kind, courteous husband to me. In truth I couldn't be…"

Again, a silly word came into her head. She'd meant to tell her mother she couldn't have been happier, but surely, her mother had always warned her not to be shallow about this world and its perils. Happiness was hard to come by, her mother had always told her.

"You are happy in this match your father made for you," her mother suddenly told her with a smile, embracing her warmly, and Judith felt relieved and grateful for her words.

"Aye! I-I know I may be fanciful, but I truly think Lord Tristram and I… that we can have a happy marriage. I just can't wait for him to meet you! He promised he'd come as soon as he was able to visit. And you'll see he is indeed a worthy man."

"I am certain he is," her mother nodded with a smile, but Judith could catch a hint of distress in her voice.

It was natural for her mother to worry on her behalf, and Judith prayed Tristram would get here soon. Once her mother got to know him, she would certainly see what Judith already saw, that her daughter could not have wished for a better husband. So Judith hoped fervently Tristram would come as soon as could be, but the weeks turned into months and still Tristram wouldn't come. He sent word to her often. At first it was tedious business at King Henry's court which kept him away.

"I am certain he will get here eventually," her mother told her with an encouraging smile whenever she caught Judith glancing despondently through the window instead of focusing on the tapestry she'd been embroidering.

But Judith caught a note of distress in her mother's voice, and she felt wary of it. She wrote to Tristram urging him to try to do away with the tedious business which kept him from her. Yet the reply she received was disheartening.

"Tristram's mother has fallen ill with a fever," Judith said in anguish coming upon her mother one evening, after she'd received the letter the messenger had brought her.

She felt worried for Lady Aelis, Tristram's mother, who had been most kind and courteous to her upon her marriage to her son.

"Don't you think it would be better to seek London in order to aid Lady Aelis in her hour of need?" she said, thinking Tristram and his mother may need her at this time.

"Has your husband asked for your aid?" her mother inquired.

Judith perused the letter once more. Tristram was worried for his mother's health and thought it more prudent to be by her side in this hour of need, but he was not asking for Judith to come and help him care for her.

"He has two sisters, doesn't he, your husband?" her mother went on.

Judith nodded. One of Tristram's sisters was at this time also by their mother's side and this was perchance why Tristram didn't feel the need to call upon his wife's assistance. And Tristram had already written that his other sister was coming from her demesne to look upon their mother.

"I'm sure then that Lady Aelis' daughters will provide the best care. And, after all, you are as yet untrained and untutored in both the healing arts and household matters," Lady Fenice added.

Judith nodded, with a slight blush. Her mother was right. Here, Lady Fenice's trusted companion, the redoubtable Dame Berthe, held the reins of their household under her mother's very distant supervision. Judith had sought to aid in this ever since she'd grown older, but Lady Fenice had assured her there was plenty of time ahead of her to learn. Instead, her mother had trained her in the gentler arts ladies should master, so Judith was a fine weaver and embroiderer. Yet it was not in these arts that her talent truly lay. She was indeed an accomplished lute player and her singing voice was very fine. She could read and write Occitan and Norman and English and even understand Latin when required of her. She well recalled Tristram had spoken to her of his own home which lay in the vicinity of Winchester, where he hoped they would settle once she felt ready. She would soon need to learn the required accomplishments of tending a household.

As if she'd guessed her daughter's thoughts, Lady Fenice nodded as she spoke, "There's time enough to train you to become mistress of your own demesne. Since I suppose your husband will one day command you to leave your childhood home."

Judith nearly flinched at the word *command*, because she was already having a hard time thinking she would ever have to leave Redmore. She loved her home and it was painful to picture her life in a different place.

"Tristram – he hasn't pressed me for it. He understood I needed to be here by your side. Just as he now needs to be by his mother's side. You do not think I should go to him?"

"He hasn't sent for you. But I am sure he will be glad to see you if you think you must join him," her mother told her, and

Judith saw again she was trying to put on an encouraging smile.

In spite of this reassurance, her mother's face was an open book to Judith, and she began to fear that Lady Fenice, who was at present feeling poorly yet again, could not spare her at this time.

"I shall write to Tristram and tell him we'll send prayers for his mother's swift recovery!"

And she did write to Tristram, hoping Lady Aelis would soon feel better and that the fever was only a passing ailment. Yet a month later, dire news reached them, that God had seen fit to take the lady Aelis from among the living. Tristram's letter held bleak news and a warning. The same fever which had claimed his mother's life had swept several households in the city of London, and it was not wise for Judith to try to join him there at this time.

"How wretched he must feel to have his dear mother gone!" Judith said with a deep sigh. "Perchance, in spite of his warning, I should go to be with him. I am safe and sound and have never been ill in my life."

Her mother shook her head though, reminding her that her husband's words were wise. He had commanded she should stay at Redmore and it would be unwise to disobey him at this time. Still, Judith disliked the use of the word *command* just as much as she had the first time when her mother had used it to speak of Tristram. But she recalled she'd never heard true command in Tristram's voice whenever he spoke to her. She paused to think upon the danger which awaited her in London. She feared less for herself than for the loved ones who now resided there.

"But Father is in London," she whispered in anguish.

Her father was in London, just as Tristram was, to attend Court business, and she didn't like the thought of both her husband and her father being in a place where sickness was beginning to spread. Nevertheless she needn't be told that King Henry's commands were not to be ever disobeyed.

It was with an uneasy heart that Judith spent the next weeks, worrying over both her father and Tristram. Yet her mother was comforting whenever Judith spoke to her of these worries.

"Your husband's young and hale. As for your father…"

Here Lady Fenice always glanced away from her daughter with a bitter twist of her mouth.

"Your father's strong as an ox. Nothing can touch him," she liked to add in a blank voice.

Yet not another month passed before more dire news reached them. The fever which had claimed the life of Tristram's mother had also claimed Judith's father. Judith stared at the unsealed letter from Tristram in disbelief mixed with searing pain.

"Father… So strong… Still in his prime," she whispered, unwilling to keep tears at bay.

"May God have mercy upon his soul," her mother said, her eyes dry. "He was a worthy man, in his own way."

Judith nodded. She hadn't known her father well, and hadn't been too close to him, but upon his death she finally understood she had truly cared for him. Now that he was gone, she fully saw she would miss him very much, even if at times he had been harsh and uncaring in his ways. She stared at Tristram's letter, trying to summon strength. Tristram warned it was unwise to join the city even now, and that he would make arrangements for a burial and a mass fit of Sir Edward's birth and rank. Judith and her mother should be at peace that all the proper ways would be observed in this time of great need.

And Judith did her own part at Redmore to honour her father's memory and work for the salvation of his soul. Mass was sung in Church, and a new chapel was commissioned, to remember her father by. Alms were given to the poor and money gifts to the servants, who, Judith understood, had loved their master well because they sincerely mourned his passing.

It was upon the third day of their mourning that Judith ventured to speak to her mother, knowing this shouldn't be postponed, "Mother, I think perchance we should inquire of father's..."

Judith was aware her mother didn't ever like the words spoken in front of her. It was known to all that Judith's father had kept a commoner in the village for his leman. And while Judith had never even spoken to this woman, she felt it was her duty to inquire about her, since her father was no longer among them. This woman had been under her father's protection and it would be uncharitable of his family not to think of her. After all, many lords kept common women besides their wives, following the older Danish customs of times past, and Judith knew this well. Yet she also knew her mother had been deeply hurt by what her father had done. No matter what the old ways were and what many lords seemed to believe, it was utterly wrong for a husband to dishonour his wedding vows, Judith thought, and her father was certainly guilty of that sin. Nevertheless, things were what they were. This common woman had lain with her father, and her father's bond to her could not be so easily dismissed.

"Your father's woman, you mean," Lady Fenice said in a hardened voice, straightening her back.

Judith nodded.

"I wouldn't worry about that one," her mother added, with a shrug and a bitter smile. "Women of her sort always manage."

"Still," Judith ventured. "I think it is only right she should receive assistance upon Father's death."

Her mother waved her hand carelessly, with a look of sheer disgust upon her face.

"Do whatever you wish. As long as you don't set eyes upon her. I suppose we should show ourselves magnanimous. I would not have it said that people of our blood are ungracious to commoners, even to commoner harlots such as this one."

Judith widened her eyes, because her gentle, soft-spoken mother never used coarse words and had always urged her to avoid such language. Her mother smiled ruefully, clasping Judith's hand.

"I know, that was unkind of me to say, but it has always hurt so – the way your father chose to behave towards me. Well… may you never get to live what I have lived! Yet I expect you might one day. Most men are fickle."

Her mother's hand clasped hers firmly, and Judith thought of Tristram and of how apart he was from other men. For a moment she wanted to believe a man such as Tristram would never be fickle. She recalled though they'd been separated for many months, which had now nearly turned into a year. And they hadn't even bedded. She was not as simple as to think a hale man of Tristram's age didn't have his own natural urges. And could she even blame him if he didn't keep faith with her while they were parted? She knew most women of her station turned a blind eye to their husbands' behaviour. Men have urges they cannot suppress, her aunt Edith had always said.

"Not Tristram!" Judith found herself suddenly whispering, although she knew it was silly of her to hope her husband would keep faith with a wife he hadn't even bedded yet.

The way her mother looked at her nearly broke her heart.

"I'm sure you have the right of it, my sweet one," Lady Fenice said, attempting to smile, but failing.

Judith tried to tell herself it didn't matter. After all, Tristram and her had not yet shared their bodies, so she couldn't hold anything of this sort against him. But why did it hurt so much to think upon him in another woman's arms? Her mother had the right of it. The pain was fierce. Although she had at first wanted to look upon her father's mistress, she decided not to do so and she only sent the gift of money she intended. It was with surprise that, a couple of days later, she found out the gift had been returned. It appeared her father's mistress had no need of it.

Lady Fenice stared through her window, as if attempting to glance upon the village which lay beyond their castle.

"See, I did tell you, daughter, women of her sort always manage. One man or several can always be found to take care of their needs."

Judith could understand her mother's bitterness, because, for some days now, her own nights were filled not only with sad memories of her father, but also with frantic thoughts of Tristram in another woman's arms. She missed him, and she wished he could come sooner, so they could start their life together and she could put her unseemly, jealous thoughts aside.

CHAPTER 9

PRESENT TIME, 1174

Judith hardly saw her husband during the day and she strived not to think too much upon him as she busied herself with her tasks over the week that passed. With relief, she saw he didn't seek as yet to change the ways in which she oversaw her household. It appeared she was still the lady of this house and of this demesne, and Tristram hardly interfered with her ruling over her people as he fulfilled the pressing duties of looking upon his men and upon the demesne's defences. In this, he had mainly to deal with Sir Roderick, and Judith was mostly spared from her husband's presence during the day. However, Judith was not as simple to believe this state of things would go on for much longer.

As the new lord of Redmore, Tristram was soon to take over several of the duties Judith had fulfilled until now. In truth, if their marriage had been a genuine one, Judith would have welcomed the presence of a husband who would share in the burden of overseeing their demesne. Yet their marriage was not a genuine one, and Judith had no doubt Tristram would not tarry to make it plain to her own people that *she* was only a chastened, repentant woman who lived under his rule. And while she'd been mainly spared from Tristram's presence during the day, she always had to deal with him at night, when it was time to seek her bedchamber.

Indeed, tonight when Judith came to bed, she found Tristram had already had a bath and dressed for the night. She suppressed a sigh, bidding the servants to empty the tub, and she waited for them to bring it again, filled with new, hot water for her to bathe as well.

The servants fulfilled their duties diligently before retiring, but Judith now felt tired and cross, and in no mood at all for Tristram. By the way he was now looking upon her, he must be already thinking of chastising her again. Judith closed her eyes tiredly, not wanting to think of the spankings she'd already received from him, and of the way her treacherous quim had been gushing wet and pulsing shamefully for his thrust each time he was done punishing her.

At this time his brooding stare roamed upon her as she began to undress, and she found herself unwilling to hold her peace.

"Quit staring, please, my lord. I wish to have my bath in peace," she found herself muttering, only belatedly understanding she was already giving Tristram further reason to claim she was in need of chastisement.

"Defiant words, since you're my lawful wife and I can stare all I please," Tristram soon countered just as she'd thought he would.

"And I suppose now you'll spank me for them," Judith said wearily, starting to step out of her gown.

Tristram said nothing, just letting his gaze linger upon her.

"Do you also plan on having to me tonight?" Judith asked, knowing already his course was set whatever she meant to say.

Again, Tristram said nothing.

"Because you can't have me tonight," Judith added mockingly, knowing he would not like at all that she was further defying him.

She stalled removing her underdress, loath to get naked in front of him at this time. All she wanted was to have her bath in peace, away from his sombre gaze.

"I did not think I would," Tristram suddenly said in a quiet voice. "Not when your monthly flow is upon you."

Judith's cheeks heated, because he was the first man to speak of such things with her.

"How do you know?"

Tristram shrugged.

"I grew up with sisters," he replied tersely, now turning his back on her to go to the window.

Judith felt grateful he had ceased staring at her. He blissfully ignored her when she had her bath and saw to the rags she'd been using for her monthly flow, replacing them with new ones. She soon felt refreshed after she'd had her bath and slipped into a clean shift. Yet, as she climbed into bed, she couldn't help wondering whether Tristram might still want to punish her tonight. Her gaze upon him must have been searching and anxious, and he raised his dark eyebrows at her when he strode to the bed. However, with sheer relief, Judith perceived he was now reaching to snuff the candle. It seemed tonight she'd been given a reprieve.

"It's best you saw the midwife in the village one of these days," Tristram spoke in the dark as he was climbing into bed by her side.

"Midwife?" Judith asked, uncomprehending.

She sat up, downright puzzled, because it had been but a few days since they'd first coupled, and she was now having her courses. Surely, he wouldn't think…

"I'm certain she will know of a brew, herbs and some such,"

Tristram went on and his voice sounded cold. "I'll have more care and will no longer spill my seed inside you, but it's best to speak to her as well."

As Judith recalled their heated couplings, with a fierce blush in her cheeks, she understood it was only twice that Tristram had given her his seed. She frowned, at first not understanding why that was, but then she remembered how the priest in her village had one day ranted in Church against those who coupled only for pleasure. He'd said both the men who withheld their seed and the women who used herbs and pessaries were certainly risking eternal damnation. At the time, Judith had not truly cared for his words, but now Tristram was acting just like those the priest had called sinful.

"Don't you wish for a child?" Judith found herself asking.

She strived to tell herself that what he'd uttered was blasphemy, but at this time, when she conjured up the image of a child they might have, she could think only of her own estranged parents and of how they'd always looked upon one another coldly. It was a strange thought, yet it came unbidden. If Tristram and she soon had a child, it would be the child of bitter, estranged parents.

"Do *you* wish for children?" Tristram countered, and his voice sounded cold.

Children were God's gift, Judith knew full well. At one time she'd thought she would give Tristram both sons and daughters and had welcomed the thought. Things between them had not been bitter then. Now Judith felt a chill run through her veins, understanding things between her and Tristram might always be just as bitter as they were now, in spite of the lusty heat when they coupled. Did that mean it was best not to ever have children?

"You will want sons. Not now perchance, but later. All men do," Judith said, making her own voice cold and recalling what her mother had taught her.

Lady Fenice had schooled her on this, saying men set little store on daughters and wished for nothing but sons. Judith had always thought this unfair. And now she remembered she'd spoken to Tristram of this during the first days of their marriage. She plainly recalled Tristram had told her he would cherish a daughter just as much as he would a son. Had he been lying at the time, perceiving this was just what she'd wanted to hear?

"All men do, you say," Tristram spoke in a voice which sounded mocking in the dark. "How well you seem to know the heart of men!"

His mockery stung, but Judith clamped her mouth shut, knowing it was no use to exchange angry words with him. She had well understood he no longer cared to hear anything she said. Yet she also noticed he had not said anything further of the sons he might wish to have one day. She suppressed a sigh, trying to chase away the heart-breaking feeling which enveloped her and striving not to think of the dreams she'd once had of a life where she would bear Tristram's children.

"Go speak to the midwife. She would know how to advise you," Tristram now commanded. "Her name's Nell Tyler."

"I know too well what her name is," Judith retorted, hissing through gritted teeth.

But how did Tristram already know this woman? Judith recalled he had already visited the village several times since his arrival, so it was plain he must have met this woman there.

"I see you wasted no time in getting yourself acquainted with the people in my village," she muttered savagely.

"Certainly. I am their lord, aren't I?" Tristram countered. "Besides, I have at last learnt to speak their English quite well."

He had. Ever since his arrival, Judith had noted Tristram no longer had any hardship in understanding or speaking the English of the North. It was now plain he'd learnt it. And she recalled the first time she'd spoken to him in her English, on one of those nights when they'd talked and laughed together and shared dreams of happiness. She closed her eyes, burying her head in the pillow and simply wanting to weep.

CHAPTER 10

TWO YEARS AGO, 1172, REDMORE

Tristram looked upon the walls of Redmore and wanted to shout with joy. It had been so long since he'd seen his bride. The turmoil caused by the killing of Thomas Becket and then the illness which had swept London had made it hard for them to reunite. And then there'd been the grief of both his mother and her father's passing. Tristram now counted no less than eighteen months since Judith and he had set eyes on each other. A long time – far too long. In the past months Henry had given him many duties, and then there had been other pressing things which had forced him to join his own demesne.

While his lady mother had been alive, she'd overseen their home and lands, but now with Lady Aelis gone, he'd had to go to Devensey and appoint a chatelain who would look upon things. Nevertheless the whole business had taken far longer than he'd assumed as there'd been many loose ends and many things neglected while he'd been at Court. In truth, had his wife's mother not been ailing, he would have called upon Judith's help to see to their demesne. She may be young and unschooled in such things, but she was clever and seemed a fast learner. He felt confident she would learn to see to their lands and home just as capably as his sisters ruled their own demesnes. However, he'd been loath to ask for Judith's help. Every letter he'd had from her had impressed upon him that her mother was feeling poorly. The pain over his own mother's passing was still fresh and he hadn't wanted to rob Judith of even an hour spent in the company of Lady Fenice. Besides, Judith was now the heir of Redmore, and the castle and lands would fall mainly upon her shoulders. He'd understood that at this time he couldn't be as selfish as to call her away from where she was needed more.

He'd been apart far too long from his new bride, but now he was here at long last, and he couldn't wait to set eyes upon her. He'd missed her. And, he admitted to himself with a suppressed sigh, he'd also missed a woman's touch and caresses. Certainly, he'd kept faith with his lady, because he'd never been the man to break an oath, but heated images of lovemaking had plagued his dreams and even his waking hours.

His face lit with a smile when he finally caught sight of Judith, waiting for him in the outer bailey accompanied by her people. And his first thought was that he should run to her and take her in his arms and carry her up the stairs to her bedchamber. Yet he restrained himself. So many people were waiting by her side, having gathered to witness his arrival. Instead of running to his wife and kissing her ardently, he made himself give her a gracious bow. She replied with a curtsy.

"My lord," she said, and her voice sounded restrained, rather than full of joy.

She proceeded to let him meet Sir Roderick and his wife, Dame Berthe who aided in the overseeing of Redmore, as well as those other people who saw to the welfare of her demesne. Tristram strived to focus upon the introductions, although his thoughts were only upon the bride he hadn't seen in so long.

At last, he caught a moment of respite and clasped her hand in his. And he simply found he could no longer care for those around them.

"Come away! Let us talk, wife – the two of us," he blurted out artlessly.

Certainly, talk was not the first thing upon his mind, and it seemed plain the other people around them had perceived this, and were already looking upon them with faint smiles. Judith blushed scarlet, and he felt truly embarrassed to have made her ill at ease. His lady mother would be tossing in her grave to think her son was behaving so discourteously.

"For privacy, it's best you seek the solace of my lady's chamber, my lord. You must have much to talk about," Dame Berthe interceded smoothly.

Unlike the others' countenances, the lady's expression betrayed nothing.

"My lady Judith," Dame Berthe added. "Perchance you, as the lady of this house, should be the one to lead your lord to the chamber?"

Still blushing fiercely, Judith nodded, yet she stepped towards the stairs and Tristram found himself eagerly following her, unable to still care for what the others might think of his behaviour. Together they climbed the stairs which led to Judith's bedchamber, and for a while they climbed in silence. They soon reached a spot where no one else could see them any longer, and where the space around them narrowed. So Judith had to lead the way and Tristram followed, because the staircase was now too cramped to fit two people walking side by side. And Tristram's eyes didn't tarry to fall on the swish of Judith's ample hips as she was making her way up. He bit hard into his lip, recalling how he'd dreamt of Judith's curves and of finally caressing her body at leisure. He must have been tarrying because Judith suddenly turned her head over her shoulder to see why he'd paused. And at that moment Tristram could bear it no longer.

He stepped up to her and simply pinned her against one of the walls in the narrow space. He kissed her hungrily, pressing his heated body against hers.

"So long," he muttered against her lips, loving the velvet of the kiss.

There was a hot urgency to it he revelled in, and he only belatedly recalled the kisses they'd shared so far in their marriage had been scarce, and that he'd mostly contented himself to brush his lips against Judith's hands and cheeks, quite chastely. He had barely even kissed her lips. And now he was kissing her wantonly, with tongue and teeth. He also became aware that one of his hands had already reached to hoist her skirts, while his body was pinning her against the wall.

He hastily disentangled himself from her, feeling deeply ashamed of his behaviour.

"I humbly beg forgiveness, my lady," he found himself muttering, capturing her hand and brushing a light kiss upon it.

Judith was now blushing even more deeply than before, and she was touching her lips, with a stunned expression on her face. Tristram cursed himself in his mind. She was still a maiden. And they'd not seen each other in so long. Instead of treating her gently and of seeking to talk to her, he'd behaved like an unfeeling lout.

"Perchance... if you will lead the way," he muttered, feeling mortified.

Judith nodded after what seemed to him like a long while. They reached Judith's bedchamber in silence, and Tristram felt grateful he was finally able to sit himself in a chair and catch his laboured breath. His heart was thumping fiercely. And he felt thankful his long tunic must hide most of his painful arousal.

"So," he said artlessly, clearing his throat. "At last we meet, my lady."

Judith said nothing, still staring at him with a deep blush in her cheeks. Tristram suppressed a heartfelt sigh of regret. He had behaved wretchedly. And in the next days he should strive to be courteous and mindful of his wife. He willed himself to temper his maddening arousal, reasoning it would be wrong to rush things. In a day or so, when Judith had taken the time to reacquaint herself with him, things were bound to take their due course. He well recalled that, whenever he'd touched her in those first days of the marriage, Judith had appeared shy, but she'd not appeared to fear his touch. In truth, on the stairs, it had seemed to him she was returning his kiss with abandon. But at this time his mind was so fevered with lust of her that he simply couldn't tell if her acquiescence had been all a figment of his heated mind. So he reasoned it was best to temper his ardour. He was too famished for her touch. A famished man might end up ill-treating a woman who was unschooled in lovemaking.

He willed himself to disregard his lust, and, as he started to talk to his wife, telling her how his journey had been, and hearing her talk in that lovely voice of which he'd often dreamt, he soon began to feel more at ease. He'd missed Judith so! And he immersed himself into the sheer joy of being with her after such a long separation. They talked at length, and she told him of Redmore, and of the things she'd done in his absence. They talked at leisure until evening fell, and at last they descended to have supper. Tristram was yet to meet the lady Fenice, who had been unwell before, but who now sent word she felt up to meeting her new son-in-law.

CHAPTER 11

*T*ristram looked upon the lady Fenice, after he'd given her a bow. The lady did look pale and somewhat older than he recalled her. She was still an uncommonly beautiful woman, graceful and poised, who met him with a serene expression upon her countenance and a regal tilt of her head.

"My lord Tristram," she said, in a sweet, mellow voice which sounded very much like Judith's.

Tristram strived to look stern, because this woman, just like Judith, had stood against King Henry and he was bound to deliver news from his monarch. Yet Henry had decided to be gracious with most of those who'd stood against him. And Lady Fenice was ailing and her family was still a powerful one. Henry was well aware he needed to show himself magnanimous, since the whole Christendom's eyes were still upon him after the killing of Thomas Becket.

"My lady," Tristram said. "King Henry has decided to be

gracious. You're pardoned for rebelling against him. Henry means to be honourable to his vanquished foes."

Lady Fenice nodded, and Tristram saw a look of sheer, warm gratitude in her blue eyes. He suddenly felt very guilty for his own part in this war. He'd been ordered to capture her castle. And he knew too well Judith's mother had only been supporting Eleanor's cause. Judith might have spurned and betrayed her husband. But Judith's mother was not guilty of any wrong against him. She'd just taken an opposite side to his, and Tristram could not hold that against her.

"I thank you for being so gracious!" Lady Fenice said with tears glistening in her eyes. "And for allowing us to still reside here!"

"Things have been harsh on both sides in this war. Rest assured, I will never bring myself to chase you from your home as long as you wish to remain here. It would be most dishonourable of me," Tristram spoke in a soothing voice, with an incline of his head.

He'd have abided by Lady Fenice's decision and aided her to rejoin her French home or allowed her to seek a convent, but it seemed that, like Judith, Lady Fenice wished to remain at Redmore. He bit his lip in anger when he thought upon Judith. Judith certainly still believed the worst of him, failing to see he had done what he'd done in order to protect her from a more dire fate. As always, she was blind to him and to his attempts to aid her. He supposed it was just as well. Since he'd chastised her in front of everyone, she had true cause to hate him. It was plain she couldn't see he'd chastised her but mildly, though he had been required to deliver a harsh punishment upon her. And it was, for the time being, perchance best she thought herself wronged. As long as his cousin was here, it must look that Tristram was a harsh husband to her. Yet it didn't help that Judith still appeared defiant rather than chastened.

"Speak to your daughter for me," he found himself telling

Lady Fenice. "Make her see that as long as my cousin is here, she must strive to look repentant for the way she behaved. I vowed for all the court to hear that I would chastise my wife for what she did if I decided not to cast her away, and I am not a man who's ever broken a vow. So chastise her I must! Until the Church and the King are satisfied I have her contrition and obedience. It's best she soon show contrition! So that my cousin would send word of it and we can all be free of his watchful eyes."

He already knew Lady Fenice was an astute woman. And, unlike Judith, Lady Fenice was a woman who saw reason. He hoped this time Judith's mother would make her daughter see reason. As for speaking to Judith himself – he no longer felt his wife deserved this courtesy from him after the wretched way she'd behaved. She'd broken her vow to him and had unjustly spurned him years ago when he'd strived to earn her love. He had no words to share with Judith. Not any longer.

"I will, though I fear very much Judith won't heed me. She is her father's daughter and quite wilful, you see," Lady Fenice said with a chagrined expression on her face.

Tristram nodded with a grim expression of his own.

"It would be for her own good to let go of her wilfulness. Make her see there is no other way! Better that *I* chastise her. And once my cousin sees she is repentant, there'll be no need for more chastisements. I am not vengeful. I'm only doing what needs to be done for us all to have our peace."

Yet as he spoke the words, he went in his head over the chastisements he'd delivered in the bedchamber, and his blood heated just at the thought of them. To him, they had become love play and not punishment, a dangerous game he found sinfully wicked and pleasurable. And he was well aware that, unlike the belting he'd delivered for all to see, the pain he'd bestowed upon his lady in the privacy of their bedchamber had been always mingled with pleasure.

He stifled a sigh, resolving not to think too much upon the punishments. They were punishments, nevertheless. And Judith would do well to submit to them and appear to have learnt her lesson in obedience. It was for her own good to do so.

Lady Fenice seemed to easily understand he was playing his own part in this dire state of things, striving to spare Judith from true pain and humiliation. It would be dishonourable of him not to attempt to shield his wife from harm, although she didn't deserve his aid. Tristram found he could never behave otherwise.

"I shall tell my daughter it's best she submit to you, as a good wife should," Lady Fenice said in her melodious voice.

Tristram let out a rueful laugh. The Judith he'd first known had looked sweet and shy and ready to do his bidding, but during his marriage he'd learnt Judith wasn't all sweetness. Perhaps the sweetness had been entirely feigned, just like her shyness.

He raked a weary hand through his hair.

"You and I both know she won't truly submit. She is most wilful. Yet tell her to use the guile she most certainly has. As long as it looks to the others I have schooled her to obedience, we shall all weather this!"

CHAPTER 12

TWO YEARS AGO, 1172

*J*udith felt elated that Tristram had finally arrived today after such a long separation. Casting a furtive glance in her husband's direction, she tried to still her thumping heart. She recalled the taste of his ardent kiss on her lips and the way his hard body had been pressed against hers on the stairs. It had been bliss to have him so close and to be kissed by him, and because of his touch, her quim had felt wet and ready. She had eagerly waited for him to claim her once they'd reached their bedchamber, and had been disappointed he hadn't done so. Hadn't he been able to see she was very eager for his caresses? Or was it that he was weary after his journey? Judith decided not to make much of this, because talking to Tristram and being with him was sheer bliss anyway. Yet she thought of the heat between them. Perchance Tristram had retreated because he hadn't been able to fully perceive how famished she was for his touch. He had always been courteous and considerate of her. So Judith started to think of the best way to show him she could hardly wait for him to bed her.

However, when she visited her mother in her chambers to tell her good night, Lady Fenice must have well seen Judith's head was on things other than their talk.

"It's plain to me you are mightily joyful your husband has finally decided to pay a visit upon you," Lady Fenice spoke.

Judith nodded, but the way in which her mother said *finally* was not lost upon her. It seemed as if Lady Fenice believed Tristram could have come sooner. Yet Judith instantly dismissed her mother's words, recalling with a smile the eager way her husband had kissed her on the stairs. He had been quite eager for her – just as eager as she'd been for him, and this night she shouldn't tarry to tell him of her own eagerness.

"All's well I hope! And I suppose I should give you advice for the bedding which is to take place tonight," Lady Fenice added.

Judith had been reluctant at first to tell her mother of what had gone on in the bedchamber between Tristram and her during the first night of their marriage. She'd felt shy of it, but she had seen that Lady Fenice had been concerned for her welfare, so she'd hurried to assure her Tristram was not at all one of those men given to brutish urges towards their wives. He'd been considerate and kind and willing to wait for her to get accustomed to him before they bedded.

"Certainly, Mother, if you wish," Judith now said rather awkwardly.

She felt loath to speak of the maddening heat in her belly and nether parts, and of the way she could think only of Tristram and of how he may thrust inside her tonight. Certainly, she would never share such thoughts with her mother.

"You're eager for his touch already, daughter, I see," Lady Fenice said, as astute as ever when it came to her daughter.

Judith nodded with a deep blush in her cheeks. Could her mother so easily tell how fiercely she burnt for Tristram?

"Have a care not to appear too eager. Men take such eager-ness to mean women are loose. And men think less upon such women," Lady Fenice said lightly, brushing a kiss on her forehead.

Judith frowned. Why would Tristram ever think her loose? And wasn't it right for a wife to crave her husband's touch?

"Men like such loose behaviour from their commoner lemans, but they expect restraint from their noble-born wives," Lady Fenice added pointedly.

All Judith's playmates had been commoners while she was growing up. She'd played with them rather furtively, because she'd known her mother disapproved of boisterous games. Yet Judith had loved those games the other children played, and she had cherished her borrowed time with them, coming to see these children were not so different from her. Perchance her mother was wrong. Tristram had kissed her ardently, so it was plain he would like an ardent response from her. Or... Judith recalled he'd hastily stopped his caresses. Had it been so because, just as her mother was now saying, she'd been too wanton in her response to his touch? And what did *wanton* mean? Was it wrong to feel so eager for one's husband? She sighed, but she soon resolved all she needed to do was to ask Tristram plainly how things stood. They talked of many things, and she felt sure he would speak to her of this and tell her of those matters he already knew better than she.

She steered the talk upon other things, yet it was not long before she came to see Lady Fenice's face was very pale, and her mother seemed to be wincing in pain from time to time. Judith knew only too well her mother's heart pained her sometimes, and this time Lady Fenice appeared to be suffering more than she had before. So she felt loath to leave her mother's side. Her mother made little of it, telling Judith to go to be with her husband, yet Judith started to feel worried at the suppressed pain in her voice. So she lingered, holding her mother's hand and talking to her soothingly.

It was perchance an hour later that Dame Berthe came to look upon them.

"Why are you still here?" she asked in plain surprise, upon perceiving Judith still by her mother's side. "What of your husband? He's surely waiting for you in the bedchamber!"

Lady Fenice sighed deeply.

"I keep telling Judith she should go to him and do her wifely duty, but the child won't leave my side."

It seemed to Judith that Dame Berthe's voice was sharp when she said, "Fenice, just let her be! She should be with her husband!"

"Why are you saying this? Can't you see I've been urging her to go?" Judith's mother retorted in a pained voice, and Judith felt it unfair that Dame Berthe should reproach her mother for a thing which was plainly not her fault.

"It is not Mother who's been keeping me. I want to be here!" Judith said hastily.

Dame Berthe scowled at her, "I am here now, and have things well in hand. Off you go, to be with your lord!"

Judith started shaking her head, but Dame Berthe simply shooed her away.

"You are to go at once. We have no need of you at this time," she said, now beginning to shove Judith out of the room.

Judith opened her mouth to speak, but Dame Berthe cut her off with a half-smile.

"Just go to him. It's plain he can't wait to hold you in his arms. So let him have his heart's desire. I daresay you'll be both happier for it!"

Dame Berthe was usually stern, and spoke but little, but her words had been spoken kindly, and Judith found herself suddenly cheered by them. She trusted Dame Berthe would let her know if her mother needed her help. So she rushed across the hall to where her bedchamber was, knowing the hour had already grown quite late and Tristram must have already waited long for her to come. Yet when she entered the chamber and approached the bed, she found Tristram already sound asleep in her bed, undoubtedly already weary from the long journey he'd undertaken to come here. He looked even more beautiful in his sleep to her, as she was able to peruse him at leisure. Hair the colour of honey, and dark eyebrows and lashes, in strange yet pleasing contrast with his hair. A straight nose and sinfully full lips. She longed to kiss those lips, but was loath to disturb him when he was sleeping so peacefully. Besides, he might not like it that she should kiss him while he was asleep. She found herself wondering what it was he would like her to do, knowing without a doubt she felt ready to do whatever he asked, because he wielded a strange power upon her.

She undressed to her shift with a sigh and went to sleep by her husband's side. She had resolved to ask him of lovemaking in the morning. Certainly, she would feel shy to do it, but they were married now and she felt sure he'd set her mind at ease regarding the way a man and his wife should behave towards one another. She soon fell asleep, exhausted herself from the excitement of this day. She dreamt beautiful dreams, of Tristram, and when she woke up in the morning, she became aware she'd been sleeping in his arms. They had plainly sought each other out in their sleep, and now Tristram's hard body was pressed against hers. He was still asleep, but his hand was now possessively cupping her breast and his hard manhood was poking hard against her bottom. Judith found herself smiling, and reached to caress the long-fingered, graceful hand he held upon her breast. Yet a knock on the door made her startle, and Tristram instantly stirred, opening sleepy eyes.

"My lady, your mother wants you at once!" a serving girl's voice was heard from behind the door.

Judith jumped out of bed, and started dressing hastily, calling for the servant's assistance. Her mother had been feeling poorly last night, and she'd selfishly thought only of her own enjoyment.

"Good morrow," she called to Tristram as her serving woman was lacing the back of her gown. "I must go at once!"

Tristram sat up, rubbing his beautiful dark eyes, and nodded. She felt loath to leave him without so much as talking to him, but it was plain her mother needed her, so she mustn't tarry. As soon as she was dressed, she raced to her mother's room. It was with relief she saw her mother looked well and was having her breakfast.

"You gave me quite a fright! I thought you were unwell!" Judith said with a shake of her head and a relieved smile.

Lady Fenice frowned.

"That silly serving wench! I told her to say I wanted to see you when you could spare the time, but she's obviously misunderstood."

"No harm done," Judith said in sheer relief. "I'm glad you're well."

Lady Fenice beckoned her.

"Since you're here, could you fetch me a half of spoon of sugar? My stomach feels rather poorly this morn, and you now hold the key to the spice chest."

Judith nodded, because indeed she now held that key, as well as several other keys in their household, chained on her belt. In the past months, her mother's health had worsened and she'd delegated upon her daughter the tasks which had been once hers. Besides, Dame Berthe now seemed quite adamant Judith should learn her chatelaine duties, saying they'd been too long postponed. Judith was glad of these lessons, but her days had become increasingly busy, because she now also had to fulfil duties which other times had fallen upon her father. Sir Roderick and their steward helped, yet there were things which needed a lady's or a lord's attention, including settling disputes in the villages under their care. Judith knew she had a full day ahead of her, although, in truth, she would have loved to idle about and spend it showing Redmore to Tristram. She reasoned she should do so, no matter how busy she was. At this time, she raced down the stairs to the kitchens, to fetch the sugar her mother had asked for. Sugar was a dear spice, and her mother had always impressed upon her the spices in this house should be dispensed only by the lady of the house.

It was upon her return, when her hand was already on the doorknob of the solar, that she heard worried voices.

"Did you hear something? Is it Judith?" Dame Bethe's loud voice asked.

"No… Not yet… Quick, I've something to ask you before she gets back," her mother's hasty voice cut in.

Judith frowned, and was flustered. She wanted to leave, because it was not like her to listen upon doors, but the distress in her mother's voice made her pause.

"How does this husband of hers look upon her?" Lady Fenice asked. Her voice was loud and it seeped with worry.

Dame Berthe laughed. "Didn't you see for yourself? He has eyes only for her. I am so glad. And such a handsome, well-spoken man! Our Judith has made a lucky match for sure."

"I do not know. You see, I've had word from my sister. She was at Court while he was there. It seems…"

Here Judith heard her mother sigh.

"From what my sister tells me, he's dallied with quite a lot of women during the past year – commoners… Noble ladies too. I fear it was not pressing business which kept him away from my daughter, but other things."

"You do not say!" Dame Berthe exclaimed in chagrin. Yet after a short while she added, "He is young and handsome and they were apart for too long. You know as well as I that many men don't keep faith with their wives when they are not with them! But now he is with Judith. And by the way he's been looking at her, I do not think he'll stray if Judith gives him what he craves. A man who is well-pleased is less bound to stray, as you know."

"Still, I fear he will, and you know Judith. She's kind and gentle and caring! Her heart's too tender, and I fear he'll break it. She cares for him already far too much, didn't you see?"

"Then you mustn't tell her any of this!" Dame Berthe suddenly spoke and her voice sounded sharp. "What good would it do her to know of it? If it is true he's already strayed, then she can do nothing about it now. What's done is done. And if he treats her right and kindly, why does it even matter if he strays from time to time? Men do sometimes. I'm quite certain mine did a couple of times or so, but I never sought to learn the truth of it. He was away on long trips then, so I've never thought to hold that against him."

"Yet Judith is different from you and so tender! What if she learns of it? What if it breaks her heart?"

Judith had heard enough. She rushed down the stairs, biting her lip hard until she tasted blood. And she ran hard – so hard she didn't even have time to perceive when she was out of the bailey. She paused only when she reached the moat bridge, to catch her laboured breath. Tears already seemed to choke her, but she kept them at bay and tried to reason. It was not as if she'd expected Tristram to keep faith with her when he'd not even coupled with her. And they'd been apart for more than a year. She must strive to understand this and forgive his trans-gressions as a good wife should. Just as Dame Berthe had said, this didn't mean he would stray from now on, as long as they were together and shared the bed.

Pulling her shoulders back, she retraced her steps, telling herself she had no right to be angry with her husband. Yet that deep pain in her heart simply wouldn't go away, as if something had crushed it with a hammer and shattered it into a thousand splinters. She tried to dismiss it, berating herself, knowing Tristram was not truly the one at fault in this. *She* was. Whenever she thought of him, she was mad with longing, as if she'd taken leave of her senses. And just as her mother had said, her heart was far too tender.

When at last she glanced upon Tristram, he seemed so immeasurably beautiful to her that she felt ready to forgive him every past or future transgression. And she understood in deep distress that this man would be able to do anything he willed with her because she already worshipped the ground he walked on. And she felt afraid of what lay in her heart.

"Oh, here you are! Perchance we may spend this day together, and you can get me acquainted with Redmore," Tristram told her with his bewitching smile.

And Judith wanted to eagerly acquiesce to anything he wished. However, she ended up shaking her head, coming to understand her mother was right. She'd already surrendered her heart to Tristram. He had every power over it. And it would hurt a thousand times more than it had today if he chose to break it again.

"Perchance another day. I've pressing business," she muttered, and her own voice sounded cold and strained to her ears.

She needed her time away from him to sort out how to deal with the strange power her husband now wielded over her entire life. Tristram's handsome face held a brief flicker of disappointment, but he soon shrugged it away.

"Of course, I understand. I'm here to stay awhile. There's plenty of time ahead."

Judith nodded tersely, loath to look at him. Whenever she looked at Tristram, she felt ready to fall into his arms, so she restrained herself, thinking upon Redmore and upon her mother as things which would give her strength to look ahead.

CHAPTER 13

*J*udith's mother was gazing through the window when Judith came into her room. Lady Fenice soon glanced upon her daughter.

"I've spoken to your husband," she said.

"Oh," Judith muttered, striving to appear unconcerned. "What was it that you spoke about?" she then added.

"Not much. He still does not know what the fate of your aunt Edith will be, but we'll learn of it soon enough. Her husband's fallen in the rebellion against Henry, and the king is angered by the part they both played in the fight against him. Yet perchance Henry will forgive her. Our family has high standing, and he's not bound to soon forget it!"

Judith nodded. She didn't particularly care for her aunt, who was a cold, querulous woman, yet she felt sorry for her and mourned her uncle who'd fallen during a siege mere months before. She'd prayed for his soul and she'd also thought of her step-cousin, hoping Henry would be wise enough to forgive young Raymond for the part his parents had played in the rebellion. It was a relief that Lady Edith's own daughter, Emma, had already married a powerful lord and was safe in Normandy. Henry's vengeance would not fall upon Emma or her husband, who'd played no part in the rebellion. However, Aunt Edith and her husband, Raymond's father, had been among Eleanor's staunchest supporters.

"We'll learn soon enough. There is, unfortunately, little we can do at this time for both Edith and Raymond. We live on my lord Tristram's sufferance."

"Aye," her mother echoed sadly. "Now Tristram bid me to tell you to forgo your defiance and submit to him."

Judith suppressed a bitter laugh. So this was how it was? It was not enough for Tristram that he'd humiliated her and continued to do so every day. Now he wanted an even more blatant show of humility. She smiled savagely, cursing him to Hell and fully recalling her abject enjoyment of both his caresses and of his spankings. He'd already perceived she panted like a bitch in heat for everything he did, and not even that was enough for him. What more did he want of her that he hadn't already taken? He'd always had her heart, and now he had her body, and still he craved for more, to see her humbled and at his feet just to get his revenge.

"It's best you appear chastened. No good can come of your defiance, even if we both know you now hate him!" her mother said in an entreating voice, and Judith nodded with a deep sigh.

Certainly, her mother spoke wisely, because there was Redmore and its people to consider, and nothing good could come of their lady defying the new lord. Still, her mother did not have the right of it. Judith did not hate Tristram. She simply could not. Because she'd always loved him, no matter how wretched his behaviour to her might now be.

"I shall strive to do so," Judith said between gritted teeth, hating herself for loving Tristram.

Later that night she could hardly bear to look upon him, but the mad, treacherous heat and her shameless desire for his touch still burnt bright within her.

"Have you spoken to your mother?" he asked coldly, after she'd readied herself for bed.

When she'd come into the chamber, she'd found her husband already dressed for the night, as was his custom. He wouldn't even undress in front of her, the fiend, certainly knowing how much she would like to look upon his beautiful naked form. And while they'd coupled several times during the last days, Tristram had never even deigned to kiss her. He was most certainly set on punishing her for what she'd done, as if her love and lust for him weren't punishment enough for her already.

"I have," she found herself replying just as coldly. "Next time, if you have things to tell me, I'd rather you told me yourself, not rely upon others to convey your message."

He arched a dark eyebrow at her.

"Wilful and defiant," he tossed. "To think once I thought you gentle and sweet. And let us not forget, we should add deceit to your flaws."

Judith found she'd had enough. Spank her he would, no matter what she did, and then he'd love her hard and ardently. There was no helping how things were between them now, so she might as well speak her mind.

"What of your own flaws? What of your own deceit?" she cried.

His dark eyes widened at her, and then they lit in sheer anger.

"When did I ever deceive you?"

Judith bit hard into her lip, belatedly recalling she'd promised to behave wisely, because she was still the lady of Redmore.

"No matter," she said wearily. "I do not wish to speak to you, and it's plain you do not wish to speak to me. So what more is there to it? Chastise me then – as hard as you like, then have me! It's the only thing you wish to do anyway, is it not?"

"When did I ever deceive you?" he called out again, dismissing her words.

And suddenly Judith felt it was too much to bear. She felt like shouting at him in deep rage and pain, and throwing at him those treacherous, heart-wrenching words he'd spoken to her all those years ago. *Tristram, you lied! You lied to me when you told me you loved me!* she cried within herself. Instead, she fled the chamber, hoping he wouldn't give pursuit. She sought the comfort of her mother's solar, knowing Tristram would not dare to come seeking her there if he wished to punish her.

And Tristram didn't come at all, but Judith supposed she would soon get her punishment for the way she'd acted. The next morning she woke up wearily, after a night which had been mostly restless, and she went about her duties, knowing she would soon get to bear the brunt of Tristram's vengeance upon her. She was aware she was behaving unwisely, but she could not behave otherwise. Fortunately for her, both Tristram and his cousin had gone to visit the village, and Lord Bertran was the only one of their party to keep her company. She found him good-natured and amiable, and knew from her earlier years with Tristram that he and her husband were good friends. Now she distinctly recalled she'd met him upon her wedding, yet she'd been so flustered by what had happened when Redmore had been captured that she had been unable to even recognize him.

She strived to put her worries aside and behave graciously to a man who had been nothing but courteous to her. Not knowing what to say to him, she inquired idly how long he and her husband had been acquainted.

Sir Bertran smiled, and told her with a shake of his head, "We were in fosterage together, and trained under the same lord. It seemed the only thing to do was to become friends with one another. At first we had no choice but to stick together, but soon we came to see each other's worth."

Judith cast him a puzzled look not understanding what he meant.

"Stick together?"

"Aye, you see, the other boys – they disparaged both of us."

Judith raised her brows in sheer wonder. She already knew Lord FitzRolf was one of Henry's most trusted advisors, and Tristram came from one of the highest-ranking families in the realm. Besides, Tristram was Tristram, always the best-looking and best-spoken man wherever he went. How could anyone ever look down upon Tristram? His skill with a sword was known to everyone.

"Disparaged? How so?" she asked.

"Well," Lord Bertran said, speaking in his mellow, good-natured voice. "You see, I was born a bastard, and it took tedious years of arguing with the Church to establish my birth was legitimate. At the time I was in fosterage, I was thought a bastard, no matter the truth of my birth."

Judith now nodded, recalling the story of Lord FitzRolf's birth whose parents' marriage had been annulled at the time of his conception. The Church had eventually relented and his bastard status had been rescinded, yet it had taken years to do so. She could see how Sir Bertran had suffered, but it was hard for her to ever imagine anyone ever disparaging Tristram.

Lord Bertran must have caught her dismay, because he added with a shake of his head, "They called me a bastard and Tristram a girl. He had been raised by a widowed mother and had no brothers, but only sisters. And he was gently bred, not rough like them, and used to spending his time with women rather than with men. Besides, it took a while for him to come into his full height and strength. At the time he was quite scrawny and far shorter than all of us. He did his growing later on, later than most."

Judith stared at Tristram's friend in sheer surprise, and Lord FitzRolf chuckled. "I see you do not know of this. It is a tale I assume he doesn't often share. It is a good tale though – the others' disparagement, it made me better than I was because I learnt not to care for their ill thoughts upon me. This taught me to rely just on myself. As for Tristram – it also made him better than he was. He strived to show them he could fight even better than they did, even in spite of his lack of strength at the time. And there is one more thing. It taught him not to be vain. You might have perceived Tristram is not vain, in spite of his good looks and wit and skill. Wit he may have been born with. Yet his skill he earned through hard work. And he grew late into his good looks."

Lord FitzRolf now gazed at her pointedly. "And he is never petty or cruel to others. Because he's learnt first-hand the damage cruelty can do. Rather, he seeks to protect those he cares for from it, even if it is at a cost to himself."

With this and a bow of his head, Lord FitzRolf rose from the table, to go to the practice field and train with the men. Judith spent her next hour musing upon FitzRolf's words and remembering a time when she'd thought Tristram the kindest man in this world. Later, she had occasion to glance upon the practice field, and found Tristram there, engaged in swordplay with his friend. Both knights seemed evenly matched and at first it was hard to tell who would best the other with the sword, but Tristram's moves were faster and more graceful than those of Sir Bertran. Where his friend was strong, Tristram was quick, and Judith soon came to understand Bertran FitzRolf's fame as the best jouster in the land might well be true, yet Tristram de Brunne truly deserved his repute as King Henry's best swordsman. She'd always thought he'd come easily into his skill, just as she'd always thought his other gifts had come easy to him. Still, it was not so. She understood he'd worked hard for the skill he now possessed. And his friend had not been mistaken. Whatever else he was, Tristram was not vain. And truth be told, he'd never made her feel plain under his gaze. Instead, at times, when she'd seen herself mirrored in his eyes, she'd started fancying herself beautiful. And she clearly recalled the night he'd told her he loved her, he'd called her beautiful. All lies – she had decided later, when she had learnt he loved another. Judith gnashed her teeth recalling the searing pain she'd felt that night, and now she simply strove to forget what had been. It was of no matter. Now Tristram had grown to hate her.

"$\mathcal{T}$omorrow is Friday. A day of fasting and prayer and of contrition. A day you should observe, just as you vowed."

Tristram sighed deeply upon hearing his cousin's surly voice. It was a voice he'd come to hate. And he decided he'd erred when thinking his cousin was not entirely a bad man. Perchance it hadn't been so when he'd entered the Church. But now Tristram hated Isidore and his malice. And he hated what his cousin said next.

"You're to chastise your wife properly! You have tarried long enough and you know it. Today she seemed to me even more defiant, casting you dark, venomous looks. It has to end! So put an end to her defiance, unless you want me to act in your stead! I have the Church behind me and I will, if need be."

Tristram found himself growling in sheer fury, "You will not touch her!"

His cousin cocked an eyebrow, and tossed out in a voice as cold as ice, "Then do your duty as you vowed! And show me that this female does not rule you."

Tristram looked grimly upon the implement which his

cousin tossed on the table in front of him. It was a birch switch, and the purpose his cousin had in mind seemed clear. Tristram was still mutely staring at it when Judith suddenly came upon them, and when her eyes fell upon the birch, it was plain she also understood its purpose.

"So," she said in a mocking voice, which sounded unconcerned and defiant.

And Tristram knew there was no return from this, because he understood too well his cousin meant to act not only due to his mad religious zeal, but also because Judith had humiliated his family in the worst possible way when she'd let it known a De Brunne had been unable to bed her. Tristram had not truly cared for the insult, because he'd been too pained over the failure of his marriage, yet his family had deeply cared, and they would not let this be, enlisting both Henry and the Church's support to punish the woman who'd offended them so grievously. Tristram's own pleas had not made Henry fully relent, even if the punishment decided upon Judith had ended up being far milder than the one his family had wished for.

"Many thanks, cousin, for this much-needed tool," Tristram made himself toss out, plastering a careless smile upon his face and picking up the birch.

He then did the only thing he could do when his cousin was staring at Judith with such spite in his eyes. He took her away from there, hoisting her over his shoulder. He felt relieved she did not struggle or protest, which made easy his way up the stairs to their bedchamber.

At last, he cast his wife on the bed, tossing the birch aside.

"Listen to me well, you foolish, reckless woman! Listen to me for once..." he started.

Judith shrugged with a gleam of sheer hatred in her brown eyes.

"Do what you will and have your revenge! I do not care."

Tristram raked a hand through his hair, because it seemed

Judith had not understood at all the message he'd thought to convey through Lady Fenice. It had been his belief that the wise Lady Fenice would make her daughter see reason, and that Judith would listen to what her mother had to say, but he had been mistaken. He sighed, knowing there would be no return from this. His cousin must go from Redmore, once and for all, and there was only one course to take. He would have to deliver another punishment – one which was even sounder than the one he'd delivered upon the day of his arrival. Yet not one which was unduly harsh, because he could not bear to hurt his wife, even if she had hurt him deeply. He reasoned he could make Judith humble and repentant without inflicting too much pain upon her. Certainly, he would trample upon her pride in order to do so, but he reasoned it was far better *he* did so now, rather than have his cousin cruelly flog her in Church for all to see.

He made his voice dispassionate and hard. "You shall be punished. At once and well punished. And, after you've been punished, you're to go down the stairs and tell all and sundry you've been soundly chastised for defying me. You are to tell them, loud and clear, that you are at last humbled and repentant."

Judith said nothing, just staring at him, tight-lipped and pale.

"It's either this punishment, in the privacy of your own chamber, or a punishment in front of all to see, and far harder than the one you underwent when Redmore surrendered!" he threatened in a stern voice.

Judith cast him a mutinous look, yet he knew her well enough to understand she would rather submit to a punishment in the privacy of their chamber. He felt relieved, but nevertheless aware he had a hard task ahead of him. He had to make her look truly repentant, and persuade his cousin he'd brought his miscreant wife to heel.

Suppressing a sigh, he took hold of the birch, knowing he would not get to use it much, but that it had a portentous part to play in the punishment he would deliver. He placed a chair in the middle of the room and beckoned Judith to him with a grim look in his eyes.

"Come here, hoist your skirts and place yourself across my knee."

Judith's eyes darted to the birch he held, and he began to perceive fear in them. It was good she now finally felt afraid, he thought in mirthless satisfaction. It would work better and make the punishment seem to her more hurtful than it was in truth.

He raised his eyebrows at her when she tarried.

"If you do not come here at once, there'll be a renewed lesson of this tomorrow at first light. And you might not wish to have a second lesson on an already tender bottom."

Judith bit her lip and for a while looked mutinous. To his relief though, she strode at last to where he was, and obediently draped herself across his lap.

"Good," he said. "I'm pleased you're learning to obey at last."

What she uttered sounded suspiciously like a muffled curse, and Tristram suppressed a sigh. To think he'd ever believed Judith was a sweet, mild-tempered woman who was shy! He tossed the birch aside, because he had no intention to use it yet, and he proceeded to warm his wife's bottom with a hand spanking. He was careful to increase the heat of his spanking gradually so that he wouldn't end up bruising her.

He spanked slowly and methodically, covering Judith's plump bottom with a faint shade of red, then going to attend to her sit spots in the same manner. He willed himself to be calm and dispassionate and not to become aroused by what he was doing, because in order for all to be persuaded she repented at last, his wife needed to see this as a genuine punishment, and not as love play. So he ignored the heat in his body as he delivered the spanking. And he ignored the way in which Judith started to stir and moan under the mild spanking meant only to warm her bottom. When he was satisfied that both her bottom and upper thighs were a faint shade of red, he began to spank hard and fast, barely allowing Judith to gasp for breath between his rapid spanks. He alternated between the left and the right buttock until his lady's bottom was a deep shade of red and she started sobbing softly. And then he mercilessly attended to her sit spots, causing her to sob harder and harder. He only stopped when her body seemed to become pliant and resigned under his spanks, and she began to plead with him.

"Please," she muttered incoherently, and Tristram felt his heart clench in compassion for her.

He hardened his resolve to have this done and over with once and for all. He paused, resting his hand on Judith's now blazing bottom.

"We're done with this part of the punishment. You have yet to feel the birch upon your bottom."

"W-what?" Judith sobbed incredulously.

"You will spend the time I decree with your skirts hoisted, facing the wall, so you have time to think upon how you've behaved towards me. Then you will get the birch," he told her in a voice which he made calm and smooth.

He knew she would find this punishment deeply humiliating, and this was what he needed at this time. As for the birch – it was more of a threat, because he would use it only sparingly upon her, and just so that neither of them would be forced to lie in Church if his cousin asked them whether it had been indeed employed.

JUDITH BEGAN TO WONDER, through the haze of her tears, how she'd ever thought there could be nothing worse than the belting she'd received from Tristram in the bailey. Tristram hadn't used his belt now, but this spanking already stung worse than the one she'd first had from him. And he'd only used his hand. He'd yet to use the birch.

She sniffed, unable to wipe her tears because she was now holding her skirts with both hands and facing the wall, just as Tristram had instructed. And she was well aware that the fiend was now staring at her with his brooding dark eyes, undoubtedly pleased with his handiwork. She didn't have to peek at her bottom to know it was crimson from his hard spanking. And the demon was most certainly rejoicing in the pain he'd caused her. While she sobbed now, understanding that no matter how hard he'd spanked her and no matter how much he hated her now, she was entirely in his thrall. She loved him, as always, like a besotted fool. In truth, her defiance of him was just a desperate attempt to resist him and the power he had over her.

"Stop fidgeting," Tristram called to her callously from behind. "You're to stand still. Unless you want the birch to fall even more harshly upon you than I already mean it."

She sobbed, knowing he'd already achieved what he wanted. She feared that birch as she had feared nothing in this world. And at the same time, there was a deep, abject heat in her quim and a shameful enjoyment of the threat he was now making. She did not know how long she spent striving to mind Tristram's stern command, yet the time spent facing the wall was even more excruciating than the spanking. She desperately wanted to rub her poor scorched bottom, but she knew Tristram would not allow her this, nor a release of the maddening fire she now felt burning inside her sex. She already understood he didn't mean to thrust inside her after this punishment, and she hung her head in deep shame, hating herself for craving his touch.

"Good," Tristram said at last when Judith had begun to think this agony would last for all eternity. "Now it is time for the birch."

Judith nearly opened her mouth to plead with him, but at the last moment she bit her lip, resolving she would not humble herself even further by entreating her lord anew.

"You are to stand just as you are, with your skirts hoisted. And you are to receive the birch upon your buttocks and thighs without attempting to run from its sting. Do you understand me?" Tristram asked.

Judith found herself almost unwittingly saying with a pitiful sniff, "Aye, husband."

"Good," Tristram said, and Judith gritted her teeth for what she now expected to be excruciating pain.

She heard the dreaded swish of the birch before she felt its maddening sting. Once. And she gritted her teeth, willing herself to be still and obedient. Twice. New tears started flowing down her face. Oh, but it burned so, and Judith opened her mouth to beg for Tristram's forgiveness because it no longer mattered she didn't think herself in the wrong at this time. All she wanted was for him to stop. And… blissfully he did.

"'Tis done," he told her tersely.

She didn't dare to move though, because she was astounded. He'd only birched her twice, and while the sting had been fierce, she understood he'd not done it as hard or as savagely as she'd thought he would. She'd thought this was only the beginning of her new punishment, but it seemed she'd been wrong.

"You may let go of your skirts and you may turn to face me," Tristram commanded.

She did just as he'd ordered, feeling a strange wave of gratitude towards him. He could have birched her mercilessly. Yet he hadn't. She suppressed a sigh as she turned to face him, still loath to meet his eyes, and knowing her face looked swollen and blotchy. Why was she grateful to him instead of hating him as she should?

"Now this part of the punishment will be the hardest to bear. You are to state you've been soundly chastised in front of all the people we'll call upon to gather in the Hall. You are to tell them you've learnt true repentance," Tristram said, and for a moment it seemed to her his voice sounded warm and compassionate.

She lingered though, because he had the right of it. Humbling herself in front of her people would be the hardest thing of all to bear. Far harder than the spanking she'd just borne.

"You will do this, unless you want all of your people to see me birch your already crimson behind in front of them!" he threatened, his voice now hard and cold again.

She bit hard into her lip, but she made herself follow him because she knew there was no choice and that what he threatened to do would be even more humbling than what he was now asking of her. She braced herself for it, striving to take her mind away from what was happening. It was as in a dream that she and Tristram walked in front of all the people that had gathered in the Hall. Judith knew only too well Tristram was still carrying in his hand the birch from her punishment. She suppressed a deep sigh, telling herself she should no longer care. They all gathered there, at Tristram's behest, Sir Roderick, all her people, Tristram's men and Lord FitzRolf who was now looking at her with a sympathetic expression on his face, as well as Tristram's dour cousin who was casting her a look of dark triumph. She opened her mouth to speak the hateful words Tristram had commanded her to say, yet she didn't have the chance to utter them.

Tristram suddenly halted her. "My lady wife has been finally chastened, as you can well perceive, and she has learnt true repentance for her deeds," Tristram said in a high, grim voice. "And she is now forgiven. Because it's Christian to forgive," he added, giving a pointed look in his cousin's direction.

And Judith saw Tristram's cousin cast an assessing look at her teary face and at the way she held herself.

"Aye," the prelate reluctantly said after a long while. "At last she looks repentant."

Tristram spoke to him with a mirthless smile, "Good. You

have spoken the words in front of all to hear. And now I want you gone. And give your news to Henry and the Church. I have fulfilled my vow."

"You have also vowed to make sure she would never defy you again!" Tristram's cousin countered.

"*She* is still called Lady de Brunne, and you should strive not to forget! I will make sure she won't either. Just as I vowed. And now you are to go from Redmore," Tristram said in the same hard, grim voice he'd employed earlier.

"Tomorrow's fasting day. And I've yet to attend Sunday Mass. I shall leave after the Lord's Day," his cousin stated coldly.

"Fine. As long as you are well and truly gone, and I never set eyes upon you again. FitzRolf will accompany you. He's in a hurry to rejoin his own wife," Tristram said just as coldly.

He then took hold of Judith's arm and led her up the stairs. She followed him without protest, still stunned and musing upon the words which had been spoken. When they went back to her bedchamber, she attempted to sit down, but she found that the sting in her bottom was too fierce.

"Lie on your belly," Tristram said, and his voice sounded warm and gentle.

Again, she obeyed him, beginning to recall what he'd said to his cousin. Tristram went to fetch something from his trunk. She cast a worried look over her shoulder when he bent over her, hoisting her skirts to bare her bottom.

"You…"

Her heart started thumping in alarm, because perchance he meant to spank her again.

"Shush," Tristram said and his voice sounded warm and caring. "It's just a salve. I promise it is soothing."

He started rubbing a thick sort of ointment onto her bottom, and Judith began to experience that shameful, maddening sensation in her quim, because her behind felt sore under his touch, yet at the same time the cold salve felt like a blissful balm upon her skin. She sighed in sheer regret when he was done, and felt a renewed soreness in her rear when he attempted to cover it with her skirts.

"Off then?" he asked ever so gently, hoisting her skirts again after he'd perceived she was in pain.

She nodded and felt grateful for the cool air upon her heated bottom.

"You will feel better in the morning. The sting will fade," Tristram said in a voice which, to Judith's surprise, sounded somewhat remorseful.

And she recalled the look of dark triumph upon his cousin's gaunt face when Tristram had brought her down to the Hall, and she also recalled how the prelate had always goaded Tristram to punish her. *And give your news to Henry and the Church.* She plainly recalled Tristram's cousin telling him she should have been forced to take the veil. In spite of this, Tristram had allowed her to remain in her home. At the time, she'd thought he meant to have his revenge upon her. But now she plainly recalled Tristram had not even let her utter the humbling words of repentance in front of all to hear. Instead he'd spoken them himself, in a challenging voice, daring his cousin to disprove his words. And he'd used the birch but very sparingly upon her, although he could have delivered a savage punishment with it which would have made her cower in front of him. Yet, in truth, he hadn't. He'd spanked her soundly, but the punishment had been bearable. Harsh, but not one to inflict numbing, mindless pain upon her.

Judith stared at her husband in sudden understanding. Oh, but she'd been so foolish! And she recalled Lord FitzRolf's words, urging her to see Tristram was not vain, not cruel and not petty.

"You punished me because they asked it of you, if I was to stay your wife. They made you *vow* it," she muttered, berating herself for not understanding sooner he'd meant to shield rather than harm her.

He only shrugged, choosing not to answer.

"Just go to sleep. The punishment is done and over with. And you've no more to fear from me, I vow."

She'd spurned this man. And she'd humiliated him by seeking an annulment of their marriage contract. Yet, instead of seeking his revenge, he'd thought to aid her. Judith blushed fiercely, berating herself for having misjudged Tristram so. He may not have kept faith with her during their marriage, but he preserved his knightly honour. And he'd thought to protect a woman who was still his wife, rather than drive her from her home and see her harshly punished by the King and the Church. Tears spurted in her eyes. And through the haze of these tears, she saw Tristram cast her a look of sheer compassion and regret.

"Don't cry. It's done and over with. I promise," he repeated in a heart-breaking voice.

Judith found she no longer cared for the fierce sting in her bottom as she turned and sat up, reaching for her husband.

"Tristram, will you hold me now? Please?" she asked in a pleading voice.

She no longer cared how pleading she sounded. What she wanted now was simply for her husband to hold her. And she understood that, even in the year she'd thought their marriage over, she'd always thought Tristram her husband.

And Tristram held her, just as she'd asked him, and she revelled in the deep, delicious warmth of his embrace.

"Kiss me, please," she urged him, in the same entreating voice.

He lowered his lips to hers, but still he hesitated, and Judith found herself capturing his lips with hers in a hungry kiss. For so long she'd dreamt of his kisses.

Soon kissing turned to tender, lingering caresses, and Judith luxuriated in them because it was, in truth, the first time since their reconciliation that Tristram was kissing her. And it was the very first time their coupling was tender and sweet rather than ardent and frenzied.

Later, Judith lay sated upon her belly, watching her husband through the same avid, lovesick eyes with which she'd always looked upon him. Yet she saw that while he'd undressed her during their lovemaking, the undertunic he'd worn all day had stayed in place.

"Will you not undress for bed?" she asked lazily, thinking that, perchance, she might persuade him to love her again after they were both naked.

He shook his head, and stared away from her.

"Nay. I am weary," he told her tersely.

She sighed, understanding he was still cross with her for wanting to end their marriage. And she felt cross with herself, although she knew that at the time she'd felt she'd had no other choice. Yet they were still bound in spite of her actions, and she still loved him. And he... Tristram may not ever grow to love her, but he had protected her and kept her on as his wife, instead of taking his revenge. So he was not as unfeeling towards her as she'd thought him. Judith resolved she would settle for this for all times – because she understood she could no longer bring herself to ever part from him, no matter how little regard he now had for her.

She looked at him with full love in her eyes, deciding once and for all not to care she was not loved in return. She brushed a kiss upon his lips, and held both his hands towards her, marvelling how graceful and long-fingered they were. He frowned at her in puzzlement, but didn't push her away, as she began to look upon his hands closely. One hand was still reddened from the spanking he'd given her, yet now she understood why he'd done it and how he'd strived to spare her from what must have been much worse.

She kissed both his hands, then noted something she'd never perceived before about Tristram.

"The little finger of your right hand… It's slightly longer than the little finger of your left. See?" she said, feeling silly, yet very happy at what she'd uttered.

He shook his head in sheer puzzlement.

"What?"

"You're flawed – truly flawed! I never thought it when I first met you! But you are. Flawed just like the rest of us! Not flawless! Not a dream come true! I see it now. And I am happy," Judith said with a bright smile.

TRISTRAM LOOKED at his wife in some alarm, because he hadn't meant to spank her very hard, but it seemed the spanking was making her act strangely. Before, she'd been defiant of him, yet now she was sweet, just as the Judith he'd first fallen in love with. He suppressed a smile, suddenly understanding he still loved the old, sweet Judith just as much as he now loved the new, defiant one. It was a thing he could not help, no matter how hard he'd been trying to tell himself he no longer cared for her. However, he was still blazingly angry for how she'd behaved. And even if he felt sorry for having had to humble his wife in front of her people, and for bestowing upon her a harsher spanking than he'd ever wished, he still could not bring himself to forget she'd coldly spurned him.

"Just go to sleep now, wife," he ordered, making his voice stern.

Yet he could not sleep, knowing he had a grim day of punishment of his own ahead tomorrow, and not failing to recall how it had been between him and Judith and how he'd never understood why she'd come to part from him.

CHAPTER 15

TWO YEARS AGO, 1172

ristram had had enough of Redmore, and he'd already begun to long for his own home, warmer and with more comfort than this northern castle. He'd strived to see Redmore through Judith's eyes, but he had failed. And it did not help that Judith behaved differently towards him than he'd envisaged. The first day after his arrival, she'd professed she had pressing business and she had avoided him. Tristram had told himself she was upset by the discourteous way he'd behaved towards her on the stairs, and he had berated himself for his barely governed lust. He'd refrained from touching her ever since, trying to engage her in talk and laughter, and telling himself that once she saw he did not mean to treat her like an unfeeling lout, she was bound to forgive him for the crude, artless caresses he'd bestowed upon her on the day of his arrival. Yet, in spite of all his efforts to behave courteously, Judith was cold to him, and had taken to coming to bed long after he did.

Tristram began to understand she was truly angered by what he'd done. So he'd tried to have an earnest talk with her.

"Judith, the day of my arrival. On the stairs. I behaved wretchedly. I see only too well I've angered you, and for that I wish to–"

Judith had cut him off with a bright smile.

"Nay, you have nothing to reproach yourself for, my lord. You've always been considerate and kind to me. It's just that Redmore takes so much of my time now! I am weary."

Tristram had nodded, but he'd seen the look in her eyes. It was sad and forlorn. But perchance Judith was right, and she worried much over Redmore. He'd seen how hard she toiled every day to oversee her home and learn things she hadn't known before, and he'd attempted to aid her in some of her duties. Yet he'd found most of the people in the castle spoke the English of the North and he had trouble keeping up with them. Nevertheless he was now striving to learn this new and different English, and he felt confident he'd soon overcome this obstacle. He'd tried to get Judith to teach him, thinking this would help regain the bond they'd shared before they'd parted, but Judith had claimed to be too tired or too busy to teach him her way of speaking.

He sighed, beginning to think there was an easy way out of their conundrum. He loved his own home and he was needed there. And he could not see why Judith could not join him there. She was his wife, and from now on they belonged together. He didn't wish to ever part from her for as long as he had. Certainly, he would go away whenever he was summoned by his liege, but once both he and Judith resided at Devensey, which was far closer to London and the Court, their life would become easier. And Judith would find it less arduous to oversee his demesne, rather than be burdened with the care of stark Redmore. Sir Roderick and his capable wife would get more aid in overseeing things at Redmore, as he and Judith could appoint several of their vassals to come to help manage it. As for Lady Fenice, she could certainly join them in their new home, and he believed the warmer, gentler climate of his home and the increased comfort would improve the good lady's health. He liked the lady Fenice because she reminded him of the wise, tender mother he'd lost, and he would never dream of having Judith part from her.

"I have been thinking," he said cautiously one day, when he'd finally been able to persuade Judith to take a walk with him upon the hills. "If Redmore is such a burden to you, perchance you might consider joining me at Devensey."

He brightened when he thought of his home, and began to understand this might be the change Judith needed in order to become his wife in truth. She would learn to know him better by getting to know his childhood home, and thus begin to see he truly cared for her. Perchance she'd learn to love him.

Judith frowned at him.

"You wish me to leave my home?"

Tristram understood he may have erred in telling her of this so soon.

"Not now. Think upon it. I cannot stay forever at Redmore," he told her.

"You've been here for but two weeks," Judith countered, and for the first time since he'd known her, that sweet voice of hers sounded sharp.

He sighed.

"Aye, and I shall stay longer, yet we need to speak of this. Devensey is my true home."

"And Redmore is mine," she countered in the same sharp voice as before.

"You are my wife now. And…" he said in a placating voice.

Judith cut him off. "I expect the next thing you'll say is that I am bound to obey you in every way and follow you wherever you go," she flung at him and her voice sounded even sharper.

Tristram suddenly felt at the end of his tether. And he didn't fail to recall the cold way she'd behaved towards him and how she'd rebuffed his attempts to mend things.

"You are indeed my wife now," he said in a voice which must have sounded high and angry. "And, aye, as my wife it is your duty to be by my side!"

"What of yours?" Judith countered.

He frowned at her, not understanding what she meant. Certainly, he had his own duties towards her just as she had hers towards him. Why was she bringing this up now as if he'd done a grievous thing? He had already begged her forgiveness for how he'd behaved, and it now seemed to him she was making far too much of his mistake. They were married after all. And he had not pressed her to share his bed, although, he knew only too well, most men of his acquaintance would not have cared to behave as courteously as he had.

He sighed, because, in truth, those men he thought about were the very same men, who, as boys, had called his friend Bertran a bastard and Tristram himself a weakling. And he should never strive to compare himself to them.

"What is it that you wish from me?" he asked his wife in plain weariness. "I do not understand you. I do not know what you expect me to say or do. We're married now. You seemed to like being by my side before. And now you shun me. We have a life ahead to share. It seems to me we should be able to speak plainly."

Judith looked at him and opened her mouth to speak, yet she then shook her head. Soon a look of longing and regret appeared upon her face. She sighed with a rueful smile and touched his shoulder gently.

"Forgive me. I-it's silly. We've been so long apart. I thought... Oh, never mind what I thought! I suppose I was afraid you'd downright forgotten me. While I-I thought only of you!"

Her voice was just as sweet as he recalled it, and his heart thumped fiercely in his chest. He kissed her tenderly, mindful of not being as ardent as he'd been with her before, but soon coming to understand Judith was not averse to being touched more ardently. She pressed herself against him in undisguised passion, and Tristram came to understand she had not deceived him and that it hadn't been his eager caresses which had made her upset.

"I also thought of you!" he told her, loath to break the kiss. "We're in agreement then. So why was it we argued?"

Judith heaved a deep sigh, pressing herself even more tightly against him, and causing Tristram to hardly wait for the time to seek their bedchamber.

"I wasn't behaving like a good wife should. You're right. I should join you at Devensey. But Tristram, my mother may not ever be able to leave Redmore! Besides, it's always been my home. That was why I spoke to you so sharply. It's hard for me to envisage myself in another home. Yet you are right. We're married now, and my place is by your side."

"Rest assured, I shall never ask you to part from your mother!" Tristram hurried to say. "As for Redmore…"

He held Judith tight against him, recalling all the stories she'd told him of her home in the first days of their marriage. Beautiful stories, which had seemed like fairy tales to him. The way Judith had always spoken of Redmore, it seemed she loved it deeply, perchance even more deeply than he loved Devensey.

"Perhaps," he said, now fully brightening, "we might also find ourselves in agreement upon this. You needn't leave your beloved home for all times. What if we both spent every other year at Redmore and every other year at Devensey? Both are fine demesnes, and perchance things would be better because we'd get to properly oversee both homes in turn."

Judith beamed at him, and she suddenly looked so relieved that he felt the need to caution her, "Have a care though. While I am needed at Court or on the battlefield, it will come only upon you to bear the burden of both our homes. Still, I hope in time things would be less tempestuous at Henry's court. I am weary of it and do not seek vain glory on the battlefield."

"Henry's still feuding against his queen and sons?" Judith asked with a sudden frown.

"Or better say, Queen Eleanor and her sons are still feuding against Henry," Tristram countered with a frown of his own, because he'd always been loyal to Henry.

"Yet Eleanor is a far greater ruler than her husband!" Judith said quite pointedly.

He stared at her, stunned.

"You truly believe so? With a king like Henry?"

"But Henry had the great Thomas Becket murdered!"

"Yet the great Thomas Becket was quite mad and would have brought the downfall of our country. He sought to enslave all of us to the Church!" Tristram countered, not caring his words might seem blasphemous.

Judith widened her eyes at him.

"T'was murder though! Don't tell me you condone it?"

Tristram heaved a deep sigh.

"Nay, not at all. Yet Becket was not the man you think he was. He was vain and had greed and ambition of his own."

"Why, so does Henry!"

"And so does Eleanor!"

Tristram started scowling at his wife, who decidedly was not the biddable, sweet woman he'd thought her at first, then suddenly paused with a smile and a shake of his head.

"We're arguing again, I see," he muttered, understanding that, after all, it did take two to argue.

Judith shrugged and cast him a brilliant smile, taking his hand

"I imagine we'll often get to argue. Didn't you say we had a life ahead of us?"

She didn't seem in the least concerned they didn't share the same way of thinking, and Tristram decided not to feel too concerned either. His wife was right, and he expected they would not always find themselves in agreement. He didn't wish for a wife who minded him just because she was afraid to speak her mind. And he understood it was a relief that Judith now felt able to do so, and not to always feel compelled to agree with whatever he said, as she'd done in the first days of their acquaintance.

"Come," Judith called to him cheerfully. "My chores for the day can wait. Let me show you why I love Redmore!"

She now looked carefree and happy, and the worry lines he'd perceived upon her face before seemed to have disappeared. He followed where she led with a smile, eagerly thinking of the time when she got to become his wife in every way.

AS SHE WAS LEADING Tristram to show him the places she loved, Judith told herself she should strive to dwell only upon the happiness of being with her husband. The rest did not matter - whether he'd broken faith with her or not. Yet she was more and more willing to believe that Tristram had not done so, because his eyes had been warm and unflinching upon her when he'd told her he'd thought of her. And even if he had broken faith with her, she did not mean to hold that against him. They had been apart for too long. But he was here now, and she meant to be a good and true wife to him. Surely, he would not think upon another woman if she strived to be the best of wives to him, even if he was so beautiful and clever while she was only plain and ordinary.

They kissed and talked and spent a day Judith knew she would always treasure. Upon their way home there was much more kissing, and Judith loved Tristram's sinfully beautiful lips upon her own, and how his hard and heated body felt against hers. It seemed at first he was more restrained than she in their caresses, and she began to feel she was too eager and too wanton. But soon, she simply forgot herself in his arms and all her shyness melted, and Tristram's kisses became deeper and his caresses more ardent.

"Well, wife mine," he said at last with a smile, tracing the imprint of his kisses on her reddened lips with one hand and the curve of her cheek with another. "I think at last I'll have my heart's desire of doing much more than just sleeping chastely by your side."

She blushed, but she met his eyes levelly. It did not feel shameful at all to want him so much. And he didn't seem displeased with her eagerness. Rather he seemed to rejoice in it, and this was setting her at ease.

"Wait for me, husband!" she told him, deciding to be bold and brushing a quick kiss upon his lips in front of the door of the bedchamber. "I only need to say goodnight to Mother. But I promise I won't tarry!"

He heaved a sigh, but let her go, saying he'd use this time to bathe, and casting her a mischievous grin when he added he might be already naked next time she glanced upon him. Judith nodded with a wide smile of her own, because she fully remembered Tristram looked even more beautiful than usual with no garments upon his body.

She was still smiling when she went to see her mother and make sure Lady Fenice was not feeling poorly and didn't need her at this time. Her mother did not seem to be in ill health, but soon Judith came to see she was casting worried glances. Judith became aware her own cheeks were flushed and her lips must look red and swollen from so much kissing. Tristram had uncovered and unplaited her hair as he was kissing her to bury his hands in its mass, and now she began to pat it self-consciously.

"So," Lady Fenice said softly.

Her mother attempted to smile, but Judith saw the smile

didn't reach her eyes. She hurried to reassure her, "Tristram… He… he is my husband," she found herself muttering softly, not knowing what to say to make her mother see all was well and that she was happy to spend her time in Tristram's arms.

"Certainly. It is as it should be. He seems a worthy man," her mother muttered.

And Judith recalled only too well her mother had spoken of all those women Tristram might have dallied with in London, but she attempted to push the disturbing thought away from her.

"All is well!" she told Lady Fenice in a steady voice.

"Aye," Lady Fenice acquiesced, but her voice sounded doubtful.

Presently, her mother heaved a small sigh and clasped Judith's hand in hers.

"Have a care! You see, I fear he is one of those men who loves games. He does not mean to do ill things, yet it might be in his nature to toy with ladies' affections, used as he is that every woman he meets should fall at his feet. He's handsome, witty, well-born and skilful. And he knows it only too well. Life seems like an effortless, diverting game to him, and when one sees life as a game, it's easy to see others just as playthings."

Judith shook her head, attempting to tell her mother she didn't know Tristram as Judith herself now did, but Lady Fenice didn't let her speak.

"Perchance I'm wrong. Yet have a care. It seems to me he likes to play games, that one. He'll toy with you because this is how men of his sort are. And I do not want to see your heart broken and trampled upon."

"But you are wrong. This is not Tristram!" Judith countered impassionedly.

CHAPTER 16

*N*o matter how hard she tried to push them away, her mother's words of warning still seemed to ring in Judith's head even after she left the solar. When she reached the door of her bedchamber, she found that two serving women had just gone out of it, and they were both blushing and giggling. Judith entered the bedchamber with a puzzled look upon her face, only to find Tristram having a bath. She understood this might be the reason why the two serving women were behaving so, and a deep searing feeling of anger suddenly stirred within her.

She stared at Tristram, trying to hide her displeasure. He'd done nothing unseemly though. Both noble and serving women were required to attend to lords when they bathed, assisting them with soap and towels. So neither Tristram nor the serving women had done anything untoward. Or had they? Judith recalled the pretty blush in one of the serving women's cheeks. The serving woman was indeed the most fetching woman in the castle, and most men here stared longingly after her.

At present, Tristram lay in his tub with his eyes closed and a look of contentment upon his face. Yet he soon opened his eyes, and smiled upon Judith.

"You're here, I see. Perchance you care to join me in the tub, my lady? The water's still warm."

Judith had already noticed her husband was not shy at all about his nakedness, so she strived not to make much of it. She'd seen that Tristram was well used to bathing in front of the people who busied themselves about the chamber, not caring if they were male or female. However, by the way the serving women had acted, it seemed *they* had most certainly cared to see their handsome lord naked.

"Oh, I see Ann's fetched fresh towels and soap for you," Judith now said, striving to make her voice light and speaking the name of the pretty serving wench.

"Is that her name?" Tristram said, and his voice sounded idle and unconcerned, but he was staring at her with dark eyes which were liquid and warm. "But won't you join me, wife?" he added, letting his eyes unashamedly roam over Judith's body.

"Ann, aye. Isn't she pretty?" Judith found herself muttering, before she could bite back the words.

"Pretty? Aye, I guess," Tristram said and his voice sounded just as idle and unconcerned as before.

He stared at Judith with ardent eyes, and heaved a sigh when Judith did not heed his invitation.

"Shy of me still, I see. You were not quite as shy earlier though," he said softly, and Judith plainly recalled the heated kisses they'd shared in the hallway and the way she'd wantonly moaned when Tristram had unashamedly caressed her breasts with his practiced hands.

"Oh, never mind," Tristram said with a smile. "There's plenty of time for you to let go of all your shyness. And many other things I can teach."

His grin was rather wicked when he glanced at her, yet, before, when he'd been caressing her shamelessly, Judith had liked this wickedness, and he seemed to have already perceived it. It was plain he now wanted to lie with her, and it was what Judith also wanted. Yet at this time she felt her shyness fully return. It was clear he was skilled in bestowing caresses upon women. And she found herself simply wondering how many women he'd had. Beautiful women – just as her serving woman Ann was.

"Shall I fetch a fresh undertunic for you from your chest?" Judith asked, not knowing what to do with herself and seeing that Tristram had already stepped out of the bathtub and had begun drying himself with a linen towel.

"Aye, if you please," Tristram called to her as he began attending to his damp hair.

Judith strode to the other end of the chamber, then opened Tristram's chest of garments. She meant to look for a clean shirt he could wear to sleep in, because it was early spring and the chamber was quite chilly. Redmore was made mostly of stone and not of timber.

When she opened her husband's garment chest, Judith's eyes were drawn by a kerchief which lay on top of his clothes. It was very pretty, with the letter B embroidered upon it with a flourish. On it lay a dainty rosary and the pressed white flower of a briar rose. Judith couldn't help but stare, because it was a lady's rosary and because the flower looked very much like the love tokens knights at Court kept from their ladies. And the kerchief also looked very much like the tokens lovers exchanged at times.

She lingered for a while, not knowing what to make of what she was seeing, and she was roused only by Tristram's voice at last asking her if she'd been able to find the thing she'd been searching for. Hastily, Judith fetched a clean undertunic from the chest, closing its lid with a thump. She soon went to Tristram and handed it to him, attempting to stare away from his beautiful nakedness. Tristram cast her a searching look, and slipped the long tunic on with a small sigh.

"There. Better?" he asked, now cupping her cheek.

Judith nodded mutely. She couldn't tell him it was not because she was shy that she so often averted her eyes from his nakedness. It was not shyness, but deep, scorching lust that prompted her to look away from him more often than not.

Tristram's long, elegant fingers were now tracing the curve of her cheek.

"We'll go slow. And gently... Aye?" he said softly, and soon bent to capture her lips in a tender, lingering kiss.

Before, on the stairs and in the hallway, he'd been kissing her ardently and boldly, but now he made his kiss teasing and prac- ticed. And, unwittingly, Judith found herself wondering again how many women he'd kissed this way. Tristram must have sensed she was not responding to his kiss, because he soon broke it. He took her hand in his and led her gently to the bed, making her sit on it.

"What is it?" he asked in a warm voice, seating himself by her side and looking at her with searching eyes.

"Nothing," Judith lied hastily, knowing her cheeks were quite flushed.

"Nay," Tristram countered in a knowing voice. "Something, for certain. I wonder how I can make it better. Perchance you wish to play a game?"

"A game?" Judith asked with widened eyes.

But she needn't be told Tristram loved games. All sorts of courtly games, and word games. They'd already played several word games together, because they both enjoyed playing with words and making rhymes. Yet Judith understood Tristram wasn't speaking of a word game at this time. *He likes to play games, that one. He'll toy with you because this is how men of his sort are.*

"Aye. There's nothing wrong with being playful in the bedchamber, so that you know," Tristram now said, beginning to caress the palm of her hand in slow circles. "A kissing game perchance? Would you like that?" he added in a lazy voice which instantly stirred deep heat inside Judith's body.

"A kissing game?"

"Aye. It is very simple. You just close your eyes and think of a spot in which I could kiss you. You tell me if I guessed right after I've kissed you. If I am right, I get a kiss in return from you as a reward," he said, speaking ever so softly.

His voice and touch were simply bewitching, and Judith found herself already breathing hard in anticipation of his kisses. She strived to find her own voice and said, "What of penance, my lord? What should your penance be if you guess wrong?"

Tristram smiled and answered in a tone even softer and lazier than before, "There is no penance in this game, my lady. It's not that kind of game, because the time's not yet right for such. This game though... I think you may find it truly rewarding."

Judith strived hard to keep her head clear, but Tristram's voice was quite compelling and she found herself eagerly acquiescing to what he was asking. She closed her eyes as they both lay on the bed, and instantly thought of a part of her body where she'd like Tristram lips to kiss her. She thought she wanted Tristram's lips upon hers once more. Nevertheless, Tristram, the fiend, certainly had other things in mind. He brushed a featherlight kiss on the side of her neck, burying his hands in the dark mass of her hair.

"Mm," he said against her hot skin. "Did I guess right, my lady?"

Judith recalled only too well what he'd told her before. He'd get a kiss in return as a reward from her if he guessed right, and, in spite of the warning voice in her head, her own lips suddenly ached to kiss him.

"Aye, husband. You guessed right," she lied brazenly.

He chuckled, and it was plain he knew she was being brazen,

yet he closed his own eyes for a kiss from her. And Judith could not help herself. She lifted his undertunic to caress the hard muscle of his chest, placing her hot lips there where she could hear his heart thumping.

"My turn now," Tristram told her in the same lazy voice, when she was done shyly caressing him.

This time his kiss was even bolder. He undid the laces at the back of her gown and then simply divested her of it, and she was left only in the linen dress she wore underneath. He slowly lifted the hem of it, to bestow several kisses right at the sensitive spot at the back of her knee. His kisses were practiced, and Judith strived hard not to simply melt under the heat of his lips. How did he know so well what would give her most pleasure? She suppressed a sigh, striving hard to chase from her mind the image of the many lovers he might have had. Again, she lied brazenly when he asked her if his guess had been right. And then she got her own turn to kiss and caress his beautiful body. He'd already stripped himself of his shirt, but she averted her eyes from his erect manhood which she had already felt prodding against her. Instead she kissed his elegant, long-fingered hands. And when his turn came again, he was even more brazen than before. He simply rained soft kisses down her belly, and Judith thought she'd swoon with pleasure. He smiled at her when he at last lifted his head to look into her eyes.

"So?" he asked. "Was I right this time as well?"

"You know you were," Judith whispered, understanding it was not a lie after all, since all his kisses were in places where she'd pictured him caressing her in her mind when she'd thought of him in her lonely bed.

She kissed his lips ardently, and they both became entangled in the kiss. He buried his hands in her hair once again.

"I love your hair – so like a mermaid's. It is a shame you have to cover it during the day. It's beautiful. Just like the rest of you," he muttered against her lips.

And Judith nearly smiled at the praise, but suddenly a sharp splinter pierced her heart, as cold as ice. She knew she was not beautiful, but only plain. Her heart started thumping with unease. Tristram's next words did not reassure her.

"And I love you, wife. All that which is you," he said, and his voice sounded full of heat.

The image of the pressed flower she'd glanced upon sprang in her mind and coldness enveloped her entire body. How could a man as wondrous as Tristram love *her*? He must be lying. And it was perchance just as her mother had feared, that it was all a game to him. A lie… And she was just a plaything among others. Tristram kissed her again, and as his kiss deepened, she perceived he was now slowly hoisting the hem of her shift. And Judith understood that, in spite of the coldness in her heart, her quim was hot and wet for him. If he got to touch her there, he would get to see how eager she already was for his thrust. And he would get to understand how utterly besotted she was with him. And then he would break her heart, because he did not truly love her. Belatedly, Judith understood she'd begun to push her husband away.

He didn't press, but rolled away from her with an astonished look in his fine dark eyes.

"And still you fear me?" he asked in an incredulous voice.

Judith sat up, bowing her head in utter shame and raking a hand through her hair. She did not know what to believe, but she so much wanted to believe his words of love that she simply wanted to weep.

"Tristram…" she whispered, feeling utterly lost.

He heaved a deep sigh.

"What is it that you're so afraid of? I thought you were so eager, but now you flinch from me. Help me see it!"

"Forgive me," Judith muttered, deeply ashamed of herself and knowing he was being gracious at a time when other men wouldn't have behaved so.

He sat up in turn, reaching for his discarded shirt and pulling it over his arousal.

"It's best I sleep on the floor tonight. I do not trust myself in bed with you at this time," he said darkly.

"Come back to bed," Judith called out, feeling wretched. "I'll strive to do better! I promise!"

He shook his head, casting her a grim look.

"It's plain you fear my touch at this time, and I will not press. We'll talk upon this later. And I will make you see you've naught to fear!"

Judith opened her mouth to tell him it was not him she was afraid of, but, rather, herself. She loved him too much and wanted him too much. While he… She felt deeply afraid he would trample upon her heart. Was it all just a game to him? Was that what Tristram was doing now? Playing the game with an untried maiden, just for the thrill of it? She shook her head, not wanting to believe this of him. Yet the hateful image of the kerchief and of the rosary and of the pressed flower came back to haunt her. She already knew it was a lady's kerchief and lady's rosary. As for the flower – the flower was without a doubt a love token.

"You do not have to sleep on the floor," Judith suddenly resolved. "I shall go and sleep in my mother's chamber. There is a large bed there, and neither of us shall suffer tonight."

She pulled her shift over her body, and didn't even wait for Tristram to call after her. She fled from the bedchamber, like the coward she was. When she joined her mother in the solar, she found that Lady Fenice was still in bed, but wide awake.

"I worried over you," her mother said, and reached to embrace Judith.

And Judith let herself be held by her mother, as if she'd still been a child. She tried to reason she was indeed behaving like a child. She should have spoken to Tristram of her fears. Surely, Tristram was not as her mother had told her he was. He was a worthy, honourable man, and he already cared for her. Hadn't he even said so? He'd told her he loved her. Fancy that – a man like him loving a woman like her! A nagging voice inside her head wouldn't let her be. It felt too good to be true.

"Mother, has Aunt Edith told you of a lady at Court, about my age or perchance older than me? A lady who perchance has a name which begins with a B?"

Her mother didn't answer for a while, but when she spoke her voice was full of anguish.

"The lady Bernadette, you mean. Yet, nay, I cannot fathom that your husband has ever spoken of her to you. He... Oh, Judith, let this be! I'm sorry I said the things I said to you. You have a chance at happiness, and Sir Tristram is proving himself to be a gracious husband, in spite of what he did when you were apart."

"Just tell me. Do not shield me from it, Mother, please!" Judith said, sitting up and gritting her teeth against what she would now hear.

"Your husband... My sweet, men have their urges. There were women at Court and out of it, your aunt has told me – women he dallied with. I didn't want to believe it at first because you know your aunt, and I feared she spoke out of spite because she wanted you to marry Raymond. But then she told me of a lady whose family I knew well – the lady Bernadette de Villiers. I doubted her words at first. Yet Edith swore on the Holy Cross she saw them locked in a passionate embrace not three months past. Perchance it is not true. The lady's married."

Bernadette... Judith conjured up the image of the hateful kerchief in her head, and of that dainty rosary only a woman could possess. And she hated Lady Bernadette fiercely. And she hated herself fiercely, for loving Tristram so. She understood only too well this was not just a random woman Tristram had coupled with. By the tokens he kept of her, she understood Tristram cared for this woman. Tristram must love this woman deeply. Then why had he lied to her this night? Why had he called her beautiful? Why had he said he loved her? Was it all a game to him? A wicked game perchance? A mockery of her? She buried her face into her hands, knowing she loved Tristram so very much that she would be content with only crumbs of his affection or even with his scorn. Yet it hurt fiercely to think he'd sought to torment her by telling her of his love. Had he no heart, no heart at all? And couldn't he see as clear as day he need tell her no lie at all? She was already at his mercy, no matter how he chose to treat her.

"I know men of his sort, my sweet. They thrive on women's adoration. But perchance I was mistaken. Perhaps he means just to be kind to you and only hide the way things are in truth. They say the lady Bernadette is the most beautiful woman that ever was."

"I did not know of her! I haven't even glanced upon her at Court!"

"She's married, my sweet. She must have been with her husband at their demesne when you were there."

Judith pushed her mother's placating hand away and went to sit by the dark window. She didn't sleep all night, just staring into blackness. When morning came she resolved to confront Tristram. She'd rather have the truth of it than torment herself thinking upon the lady Bernadette and the love tokens she'd perceived.

CHAPTER 17

*A*t dawn, when Judith went in search of Tristram, she found him already in the stables, seeing to his horse. He wore a look of grim preoccupation on his face, and at first she thought he was still cross with her for the way she'd behaved last night. He spoke urgently when he caught sight of her. "There's need of me as soon as can be. King Henry summons me. The journey will be long and I mustn't tarry. Trouble and strife are ahead – I cannot shirk from it though."

He looked grim, yet resigned he must go when his liege called, and Judith knew at once it was a summons he could not ignore. So she assisted him with hasty travel preparations, knowing this was not the time to speak of the troubles which plagued her. When it was time for him to leave, Tristram sighed deeply, frowning upon her, and brushing a quick kiss upon her cheek.

"I gave you a reprieve last night, my lady. But this has to end. I'll make you my wife in truth when next we meet," he spoke.

His tone was one of terse command, and somewhat unlike the gentle, courteous Tristram she'd come to know, but she could understand why he was behaving thus. He had grim, urgent business ahead of him and little time to tarry.

"You'll see there's naught to fear! I'll show you. When you come to me, we shall be together!" he added in the same decisive voice which left no room for argument.

"Come to you?" she asked, not understanding.

Tristram nodded.

"After my business here in England is done, Henry has ordered me to go to France. To Poitiers and Queen Eleanor's Court of Love. He has a message for his royal wife which cannot tarry, and I'm the one he has appointed to deliver it."

"France?"

"Aye," Tristram nodded. "This time, I won't be parted from you. I'd like you to come with me. It's not an arduous journey, and I daresay you'll come to like Eleanor's Court of Love."

Certainly, everyone knew that in Poitiers Queen Eleanor had surrounded herself with the worthiest troubadours in the world. It was the place where the most wondrous songs and tales were wrought, and Judith had always longed to see it. Yet the excruciating, maddening jealousy and mistrust returned in full force. Besides, Tristram was commanding her to go with him when he knew too well she could not leave her mother.

As if he'd read her thoughts upon her mother, Tristram told her, in the same firm voice which held perfect assurance, "I've spoken to Lady Fenice in these past days. She has confessed to me she has felt better in the last months, and she has told me herself she does not need you by her side at all times. Besides, Dame Berthe is here and she will take good care of your mother while we're away."

"Tristram, I–"

Tristram shushed her with a light kiss on her lips.

"It's best this way. You will soon learn to see it is a wise course to take. You'll leave behind your childhood home for a while, only to return to it. So that you can come back a woman."

Judith widened her eyes at him, understanding he still chafed because she'd rebuffed him last night, and still thought her a child for acting the way she had. Was it because he still thought her a child that he thought he could lie to her and toy with her affections? Or perchance she was truly acting like a child and her fears were silly and ill-founded.

He bowed and kissed her hand, without delay, telling her time was growing late already and that he shouldn't linger, yet adding with a determined sparkle in his beautiful eyes, "I will have you vow you'll come to me when I summon. I am done waiting and I need you by my side."

His voice was commanding, but his eyes were warm, just as warm as they'd been when he'd told her he loved her.

"I…"

"Promise me, Judith!"

And Judith, who already knew she could never refuse anything in this world to Tristram, found herself nodding under his compelling stare.

"Aye, husband. I vow."

"Good. I shall soon call for you," Tristram said with a warm smile, which nearly made her melt, as he was mounting his horse.

Later, Judith watched upon Tristram and his men riding away from Redmore, and had a deep heart-breaking feeling in her chest that perchance he would never return and that they might never see each other again. She laughed mirthlessly, shaking her head, and knowing her fears were silly. Tristram had actually commanded she'd join him soon, and she had been too swept away by the spell he worked on her to tell him nay.

"He's asked me to go to France with him. To the Queen's Court in Poitiers," she told her mother later, as they were having a meal in Lady Fenice's chambers.

"It's well then," Lady Fenice answered. "France is such a beautiful place. Compared to it, England is ugly and dismal.

Certainly, you should go and do just as your husband commanded."

Judith sighed, not liking to recall that Tristram had spoken to her in a forceful voice, and that he'd not allowed her to argue with him. So far he'd never behaved thus to her, but she supposed she herself was to blame for it, for pushing him away as she had. She tried to reason it so. However, the excruciating pain in her heart over what she'd perceived in his garment chest returned in full force. Right after he'd left, she'd searched for the kerchief in some of the belongings he'd left at Redmore, and had soon found he'd taken it with him, together with the rosary and the pressed flower. It was plain these things had great value for him.

"If you're with him, he is less bound to stray. Though you need to have a care. I know you, daughter, and you've already given him your heart. Make certain he doesn't get to trample upon it, just as your father trampled upon mine!"

Judith opened her mouth to protest that the Tristram she knew would never do something like this. Yet did she know the true Tristram? In her eyes Tristram was simply flawless – the man of her dreams, and it seemed as if she'd conjured him up. She already loved him so madly that she was blind as far he was concerned. Perchance her mother was able to see the truth when she wasn't.

"Mother, I've given him my heart already. Besides, we're bound. He is my husband. What is done cannot be undone!"

Lady Fenice sighed, then cast her daughter an uncertain glance.

"Last night, you didn't bed…" she spoke.

Judith blushed scarlet, and shook her head. Her mother had always been able to tell such things of her.

"Well then," Lady Fenice said, speaking in a soothing voice. "Perchance…You see, a marriage can be annulled if the bride and groom haven't bedded. I've seen it done. You're not his wife in truth yet."

Judith widened her eyes. What was her mother saying? But she had given her pledge to Tristram! Besides, she loved him as she hadn't loved anyone in this world. Even if he only meant to be cruel and toy with her, she could never give him up.

"Nay! I will not break my pledge to him. Besides, I've vowed to do as he asks. I've never broken a vow."

"Certainly, my sweet. I understand, and I will not speak of it again," her mother said in a soothing voice. "I understand you want to keep a vow you made to your husband. It is an unfair world we live in though. They call us women, fickle, although we keep our vows. Yet men – they break their wedding vows and other vows to us all the time."

Judith stared away from her mother. Now that Tristram was gone and she was no longer under the spell of his beauty and of his compelling voice, it seemed to her that her mother had the right of it. She now felt certain Tristram had broken his wedding vows. And it hurt too much to think upon him loving another, because she loved him far too much. She loved him so much it was unseemly. It was torture to love him, and now know he could never love her in return. It was excruciating martyrdom to know he'd lied to her – a lie so beautiful she simply wanted to believe it in spite of it being just a lie. He'd spoken to her of love, but it was plainly all a game to him, because Tristram was in truth a man who loved games. She buried her face in her hands, beginning to wonder whether it would not be best to try to sever the bond she had with him. This way, she would never feel this excruciating pain and doubt. This way, she would be free of him and of the strange power he already wielded over her.

Tristram descended the stairs of his London home skipping the steps as he went. Today was the day when Judith would arrive, and in a few days' time they would board a ship to go to France on his mission for the king. And Judith would go with him, reluctant as she'd been to leave her home and her mother for a while. Yet, as reluctant Judith may be to leave, Tristram remembered clearly she'd told him she'd always dreamt of visiting Eleanor's Love Court in Poitiers. And no wonder. Judith made songs which were as good as those of the best troubadours in this world. In truth, she was already a troubadour, although she was too modest to ever call herself so, and Tristram wished for her to visit this court, and meet with those who could duly praise her verse. He already knew she would feel encouraged by the praise, and once she felt happy and secure, she would let go of the strange fears which prevented her from being his wife in every way.

He descended the stairs with a smile, already hardly waiting to glance upon Judith, but his eyes did not fall upon his wife, but upon a flustered man who was extending a sealed letter towards him.

"My lord," the man bowed hastily.

Tristram's heart already began to thump in fear. Had something happened to Judith? Or had her mother been taken ill? He didn't tarry to take the letter and he saw with relief it bore Judith's seal. At least she was safe and sound, and nothing unforeseen had befallen her on her journey here. He recognized her penmanship at once and, unlike all other Judith's letters, this was quite short.

My lord,

Pray forgive me. I cannot come to France with you and I cannot remain your wife. Being married to you now seems a fate worse than

death. I have petitioned the Church for an annulment, since we were
never in truth man and wife.

    Your humble servant,
    Judith of Redmore

TRISTRAM STARED AT THE WORDS, beginning to tell himself it was all a bad dream, and shaking his head in sheer disbelief, as the words started dancing in front of his eyes. He spent hours just trying to make sense of what he'd read, torn between numbing grief and searing anger. Evening came, and so did his friend, Bertran FitzRolf who looked grim and troubled.

"You've heard then?" Bertran tossed out abruptly, glancing upon Tristram's pale face and darkened eyes.

He didn't ask for Tristram to answer.

"You need to prepare yourself for their scorn. They're all laughing now, all of them gleeful!"

"Laughing?" Tristram asked numbly, unable to comprehend what his friend was saying.

"You haven't heard then yet," Bertran said with a deep sigh. "It is your wife. She asked for an annulment of your marriage. On grounds of non-consummation."

Tristram had heard enough. He let out a bitter laugh, shaking his head.

"What is she saying? That I have been unable to bed her?"

Bertran cast him a look filled with pity.

"The lady didn't offer any details. She just wrote that you and she had been long parted and had not truly bedded and, as such, the marriage contract could be voided. Yet you know how malicious people are. Now they are savouring the news with zest. And some of them are saying she's only lying, since you've been wed for nearly two years already. While others…"

"Oh, let me guess. Others are calling my manhood into question. They brand me a weakling just as they first did when we were knights-in-training," Tristram tossed out, speaking savagely.

He rose to his feet with a grim expression on his face.

"My lady wife will certainly rue the day she did this! And she will rue the day she broke her pledge to me! Tomorrow, at first light, I shall be heading for Redmore!"

"You're summoned before Henry on the morrow," Bertran said with a grim shake of his head. "He wants to hear of it. And he's already angry, saying he had never expected you would be unable to keep a wife and rule her. He would certainly ask you for the truth, in front of all to speak."

Bertran cast Tristram an uncertain glance, now raking a hand through his thick brown hair.

"Tristram, what is the truth? I've known you for a long time. And you seemed so taken with your bride. What came to pass?"

"I do not know," Tristram said, beginning to feel his temples pound hard with pain.

"You did bed her though, didn't you?" Bertran asked cautiously.

Tristram laughed to himself, knowing he would have to speak the truth in Court and that tomorrow everyone would scorn him. And Henry would be furious with him, because, at this time, Henry knew that war with Eleanor was bound to break out at any time and none of his vassals should look so weak.

"I didn't. And I cannot lie about it. They'll make me swear an oath and I am not foresworn."

Bertran sighed deeply.

"I do not understand why you acted as you did, but you must have had your reasons for not bedding your wife. Yet not everyone knows you as I do. They'll scorn you and humiliate you for it!"

"I know only too well," Tristram said bitterly.

At this time he grieved not so much for the deep humiliation he would bear, but for the way his wife had acted towards him. He had given her his heart and she had spurned and betrayed him. She'd broken not only her pledge to him, but also the vow he'd asked her to make to come with him to France. Would Henry still want him to deliver the message to Eleanor? At this time, Tristram found himself no longer wishing for it, although it would be even more shaming for him to have his mission taken away from him. What he wished was that he would be free to go to Redmore and make Judith take back every word she'd written in that hateful letter.

CHAPTER 18

PRESENT TIME, 1174

*T*he next morning Judith woke up to find her husband gone from her bed and already dressed for the day. She recalled last night's events and how she'd finally understood he did not mean revenge. Instead of avenging himself on her, Tristram had attempted to shield her from harm. In light of what she now understood of him, she could well see the punishments he'd delivered had been but mild. And, truth be told, he'd not been harsh to her apart from the humiliating belting in the bailey and the sterner punishment she'd received last night. She resolved to have words with him, to beg forgiveness for how she'd misjudged him. Yet he only stared away from her with a sombre expression on his face.

"There's nothing I wish to talk to you about at this time," he said grimly.

"Please, husband," Judith found herself pleading.

He turned to face her, and gave a short mirthless laugh and a shake of his head.

"I see. The punishment worked this time, and you seem sweet and subdued, when before you were just defiant and spiteful. But no wonder. You're used to acting like a selfish, spoilt child. So certainly the spanking served its purpose, but I do doubt you'll be able to behave for long. Soon you'll start acting just as you did. With no regard for others or of how you can hurt them through your deeds."

Judith hung her head in shame, because she'd often thought upon what she'd done. She had been too hasty in her wish to sever her ties with Tristram, and, on her mother's advice, she'd sent the letter right after she'd made up her mind. She'd had misgivings the moment the messenger had left, but what she'd done couldn't be called back. She'd tried to tell herself she had done right. And she had become persuaded Tristram would only have trampled upon her heart if they'd stayed married.

Now she became aware of the bitter, pained way in which Tristram was gazing at her.

"Tell me, husband, what occurred after I sent you the letter and asked the Church for an annulment?"

"Oh, don't you know? Don't you already know I was made a laughingstock in front of the entire court? A man unable to bed his bride? Less than a man!"

Judith blanched.

"I didn't mean for this to happen! I didn't lie and say you'd been unable to bed me. All I said was that we'd long been apart and we hadn't had the chance to be proper man and wife!"

"Yet everyone knew we'd shared a bed on our wedding night. What did you think they'd say?" Tristram asked in full bitterness.

"I…"

Judith blushed scarlet with shame. Tristram had been courteous and hadn't ravished or pushed her as, surely, other men would have done, feeling entitled to claim their wives whether they were willing or not. And this was how she had repaid him.

"I-I didn't think," she muttered, understanding it was just as he'd said.

"Plainly, you didn't," Tristram retorted tersely.

He turned his back on her.

She had been selfish. She'd thought only of herself and of her own jealousy, disregarding how her deeds might harm Tristram and his standing at Court. All she had cared about was her own pain over him loving another woman.

"But the Church refused to grant the annulment. Why?" Judith found herself asking in a small voice.

If he wanted to spank her now even harder than last night, he would be within his rights to do so, she thought. Tristram turned to scowl at her.

"Henry still needed me and he needed Redmore, knowing his feud with Eleanor might soon turn into war. He wanted our marriage to stand and he stalled for time, sending me to France to ask Eleanor to join him for Young Henry's pending nuptials. In the meantime he was able to persuade the prelates to do his bidding. And then… Well, you know only too well that Eleanor came to Court to see Henry for a brief while, yet things became worse rather than better. The war started soon after and you obviously took Eleanor's side just because I stood for Henry. Certainly, you resented it that your petition had been rejected, and sought to add further betrayal to what you did."

Judith shook her head, hurrying to say, "That, I'm not guilty of! I didn't know, Tristram. I thought… I truly thought the Church had granted the annulment. I took up the cause which seemed fair to me. I did not mean to stand against *you*!"

His dark eyes became stormy.

"Stop lying, wife!"

"I am not lying! And I still kept the letter in my chest – the sealed letter I received telling me the Church had ruled and that we were no longer wed!"

Judith didn't wait for him to say anything, but ran to the

small chest where she kept her letters. She soon found the letter, because it was a letter she'd read many times. For a while after it had first arrived, she'd read it every day.

"Here. See for yourself!" she said.

Tristram reluctantly took the parchment from her, but then he began looking at it with widened eyes and a shake of his head.

"It looks like the bishop's seal, and the words ring true, but I know for certain the Church didn't grant your petition. I was there when the ruling took place."

"Then how did this come to be?"

Tristram closed his eyes, tiredly.

"Treachery, for certain. There were many people who wanted a stronghold like Redmore to stand against Henry in the war with his sons and his wife. It no longer matters though. None of this matters anymore. You're still foresworn. You broke your vow to me. Can you deny that?"

"No, I cannot deny it," Judith said quietly.

"Why?" he suddenly asked, now staring away from her. "I've spent months wondering! Why, Judith?"

Judith opened her mouth to speak, but at this time she grasped that what she would say might anger him further. Yet speak the truth she must now, no matter the cost. However, Tristram perceived her hesitation and he laughed savagely.

"Oh, maybe you do not even recall! Perchance you did it on a mere whim. Because it seems this is how you govern your life. On whims. Or perchance you did not wish for a courteous, gentle husband. You wished for a different kind of man. One who will chastise you at every turn when you do not mind him. So I suppose this is why now you look upon me with such sweetness. Well then, my lady, now you have him!" he called out with a mocking smile on his lips, pointing at his chest.

The next words he uttered were spoken in a tone seeping with even more bitterness. "You have been well bedded and well chastised, so I suppose I am a weakling no more."

And Judith now recalled what Lord FitzRolf had told him of the cruel taunts Tristram had received in his childhood, and of how he'd overcome them. She saw now how hurt he must have been by the scorn he'd received just because he'd treated her gently. At the time she'd foolishly believed he was just toying with her, but now she saw only too well Tristram was truly honourable. And he'd behaved honourably to her, although he must still love another.

"Husband," she called out in a soothing voice, reaching to touch his shoulder.

He flinched away from her, and looking more closely upon him, Judith noticed he was wearing a strange garment below his tunic. When she gazed even more upon it, she came to understand, with widened eyes, that it was a hair shirt. It was a garment of penance which overzealous men of the Church wore sometimes. Thomas Becket had worn one, because he was overly pious. However, she'd never known Tristram to be overly pious. Rather, he scorned those who displayed too much fervour, just as he'd scorned Thomas Becket. Yet a hair shirt was sometimes worn by lay people in penance for their sins.

"A hair shirt," Judith said, shaking her head and knowing that this thing must already chafe upon his skin. "Why are you wearing this?"

"I wear it for my penance every Friday," Tristram retorted tersely.

"Penance? What for?" Judith asked in sheer anguish.

"Oh, wouldn't you want to know," he said with a mirthless laugh as he began to draw away from her.

Judith called after him, but he didn't heed her, and she remained staring after him. The letter she'd shown him lay discarded on the floor, and she picked it up. She dressed with care, aware that, after yesterday's chastisement, all eyes would be on her. At morning Mass, she strived to keep her eyes downcast, now understanding that Tristram's cousin still kept close watch of her. Her bottom still felt sore, but she understood the salve Tristram had applied had lessened the sting so it was bearable and not too much of a discomfort. She thought of his own discomfort at wearing the hair shirt, and spied his pale, tight face. He wouldn't look at her at all, and after Mass, he went away without sparing anybody a single glance.

Judith stared after him, with a sigh, yet she strode purposefully to Isidore, because at this time there was a question she needed to ask him.

"A word," she said.

He stared at her with cold, disdainful eyes.

"A bold woman you still are. You seek to speak to me? What for?" he said.

Sir Bertran was approaching and it seemed his gaze held worry for Judith in its depths. He stood behind her, in a protective stance, and Judith felt grateful for his care.

"Here. Read this. It is the letter I received more than a year ago. I thought the annulment of my marriage had been granted," she uttered glancing at Isidore levelly.

Isidore scowled, but he reluctantly perused the letter she was extending towards him. His scowl deepened when he looked at the seal.

"And when was this delivered?" he asked.

"I told you. Eighteen months ago already, by a messenger in a monk's garb."

Lord FitzRolf took hold of the letter, looking even more closely upon the seal.

"It does look like the Bishop of Canterbury's seal. Yet it cannot be!"

Isidore heaved a sigh.

"It's plain the letter is forged. The seal resembles the bishop's seal quite closely. It is not the same seal though. And what does that prove? You are still married to my cousin, though, for the life of me, I cannot understand why he would want to keep as his wife a woman such as yourself," he tossed out at her in sheer scorn.

"Oh, it proves something though," Lord Bertran countered. "That Lady Judith did not mean to stand against her lawful husband when she rallied herself to Eleanor's cause. So she is not guilty of what she's been accused! Though she received chastisement for it."

"You see then," Judith said in a level voice, searching Isidore's eyes. "I did not stand against my husband. Henry and the Church should learn of it. I have not betrayed my lord!"

FitzRolf inclined his head in grave acknowledgement, but Isidore shrugged, casting both her and the lord a look of sheer venom. He did not deign to speak to Judith though, but only addressed FitzRolf, "She might have forged the letter herself!"

"You truly think so?" Lord FitzRolf said, cocking an eyebrow.

Isidore looked plainly uncomfortable under the lord's steady stare.

"It's of no matter now. She's already been chastised, as all wilful wives should be from time to time. And far too mildly, I am certain," he growled, yet he began to draw away from them.

"May I keep this?" Lord Bertran asked with a preoccupied look on his face as he gazed upon the parchment. "I will show it to Henry!"

Judith nodded, handing it to him. She'd held on to it for far too long, and now the letter looked simply hateful. It was a reminder of the wretched way in which she'd acted towards Tristram. And Tristram…

"Sir Bertran, why does my husband wear a hair shirt today?" she asked in anguish.

Lord FitzRolf cast her an unfathomable look.

"You'll have to ask him that yourself, my lady."

CHAPTER 19

$\mathcal{T}$he bells had been still for some time and Sunday Mass was over. Tristram told himself he should feel relieved as he accompanied his cousin out of the village church. His cousin had insisted upon spending his last day in the village to see upon the spiritual welfare of its inhabitants. It seemed plain Isidore was now mad with both religious zeal and scorching ambition, and Tristram felt sheer relief that the churchman would be soon gone from Redmore.

Upon going out of the church, he chanced upon a woman from the village whom he was already acquainted with. He'd spoken to her some time ago. She was the village midwife, but she was skilled in all kinds of herb remedies. Tristram had asked her for a salve to soothe the skin. The scars left by the whip he'd had to bear a few weeks ago had mostly healed. Yet he had known he would have to observe the further penance the Church had decreed upon him every Friday until Lent, and he'd asked the midwife in advance for something soothing. Two nights ago he'd used much of the salve on Judith's sore bottom. And he needed more of it for his own back.

"Well met, Nell Tyler," he called to the woman who now curtsied in front of him.

He spoke to her of what he wished for, promising her to pay even more coin than he had last time, because, by the way Judith had held herself this morning, it seemed the salve was indeed soothing.

"Oh, so you've already used up the one I gave you not so long ago?" Nell Tyler asked with arched eyebrows.

"Not all of it, yet some," Tristram conceded.

"And what might you have used it on? Your lady wife's sore bottom from the birching you gave her?" Nell asked pointedly.

Tristram heaved a sigh, because it seemed the servants' gossip had already spread through the village, and everyone had gotten wind of their lady's chastisement.

"Aye, it is as you say. And what of it?" he said with a shrug, striving to look unconcerned.

Nell Tyler was a bold, plain-spoken woman, he'd perceived that ever since they'd first met. Yet he found himself liking her, in spite of her boldness to him.

"As long as you're not harsh again and you're a kind, loving husband, I suppose I can aid you with what you seek," Nell Tyler said, narrowing her eyes at him.

She now looked closely upon him, and at the way he held himself.

"Though I can see it is not for your wife that you seek the salve. I know the look of a man who's still suffering from the harm of the whip. You were flogged, and not so long ago. Does your back still pain you?"

Tristram widened his eyes at her, because he'd not told this woman what he needed the salve for and it seemed uncanny she should know this just by merely looking at him. Nell Tyler smiled faintly.

"It's just a gift for healing. It runs in my family, yet..."

She cast a sharp glance over his shoulder. Tristram himself

looked over his shoulder and now saw Isidore approaching them.

"Don't tell that one! He's evil," Nell Tyler said, but she spoke the words loud and not softly.

She drew away from them, and Tristram felt thankful Isidore could not understand the English of the North. Unlike Tristram, Isidore barely spoke English at all. He'd always refused to learn what he called a coarse language, although most of Tristram's large family used English among themselves in their household.

"What did she say?" his cousin asked in Norman, staring hard after Nell Tyler.

"Nothing of any matter," Tristram replied tersely.

"She has the look of a witch," Isidore now muttered.

And Tristram felt the blood rise within his temples, and that same sickening feeling which had seized him whenever he'd caught his cousin glancing upon Judith. Nell Tyler was right. His cousin was sheer evil.

"She's none of your concern. Nor is my wife. Not any longer. I want you gone at first light!" he said, laying stress on every word.

Isidore cast him a long look which held vexation mixed with wonder.

"I never understood why you let yourself be flogged for a woman who spurned you. He must be mad, I thought. Or perchance she is a witch – a northern witch, just like the one we saw!"

In but an instant, Tristram's hand went to the hilt of his sword. He held his cousin's gaze, meaning him to see the menace in his eyes.

"You think all women are witches. I wonder why you hate them so? Nevertheless, it's no longer my concern. I warn you! You are to go from Redmore and never set eyes on Judith or this village ever again!"

Isidore bristled.

"You're threatening me? Your own cousin? A man of the Church?"

"I am," Tristram said in a resolute voice, still holding his cousin's gaze.

Isidore soon lowered his eyes, yet before he did so, Tristram perceived the gleam of fear which now shone there.

"You're lost! Your soul is lost. You've doomed yourself already," Isidore snarled, but his voice sounded trembling and defeated.

"You are the one who's lost. And I shall pray every day never to set eyes on you again," Tristram countered.

When their horses had been fetched, they rode to Redmore in utter silence. Come evening, Isidore went to the chapel for his prayers, while Tristram joined Bertran for a cup of wine in the Hall. His friend would accompany Isidore to report to King Henry on how things had gone at Redmore. And FitzRolf certainly meant to share with his king the forged letter Judith had shown them. Tristram supposed he should feel relieved his wife's treachery had not been such as he'd thought, yet he did not. He felt forlorn and hollow.

"Still sleeping in the Hall on a pallet?" Bertran asked Tristram with a cocked eyebrow.

Tristram only nodded.

"She turned you away from her bed, huh? Still angry over the spanking you bestowed?" Bertran went on.

"Nay. *I* now choose not to share her bed," Tristram said pointedly.

Bertran smirked.

"You are a fool!"

Tristram sighed deeply and cast his friend a reluctant smile.

"Over her, aye. Always!"

"But have you ever told her you love her?"

Tristram closed his eyes in full bitterness.

"Yes. Years ago. She spurned me."

"But it's not spurn I see in her eyes whenever she looks upon you. It's plain to everyone that she…"

Bertran closed his mouth shut, not finishing what he'd meant to say, and muttering instead, "A blind man would see it, yet, plainly, not you."

Tristram looked at his friend in sheer wonder.

"What?"

"Never mind. I expect you'll understand it for yourself soon enough," Bertran said with a smile, and patted Tristram on the back.

"Careful! It's still tender from the accursed hair shirt," Tristram cautioned his friend with a scowl.

"You've had worse and you survived," Bertran countered callously, adding another pat to his friend's back, yet lighter than the first.

"Bastard," Tristram hissed between his teeth, but smiling faintly as he did so.

"Weakling," his friend countered with a good-natured grin.

CHAPTER 20

*J*udith had waited half the night for Tristram to come to their chamber, but she'd at last understood that, as the night before, he no longer wished to be near her. And she understood there was no choice but to seek him out and speak the truth once and for all. She would reveal to him her reasons for wanting to end their marriage. And she would listen to what he had to say even if he would acknowledge he loved another.

She sought him out and at last found him in the chapel. His head was bowed in prayer, and in the light coming from the stained-glass window, he looked as beautiful as an angel. In his hand he held a rosary she knew only too well and, Judith noted, with a stab of pain in her heart, that kerchief with the embroidered letter B. So even now he prayed for his lady love at Court – the lady Bernadette…

Judith stormed out of the chapel, then pressed her back on one of the stone walls outside, knowing it was unseemly to harbour such frantic, jealous thoughts. Yet she couldn't restrain herself, and when Tristram finally emerged out of the chapel, she found herself speaking, unable to hold off the venom which had built within her all these years, "And still you think of her!"

Tristram first cast her an astonished glance, then he shook his head. His beautiful dark eyes were filled with deep grief, and even in spite of her jealousy, Judith thought to caress his long eyelashes and try to brush away the hurt from his eyes. She loved him too much. And she couldn't bear to see him in pain, even if that pain was over another woman.

"I do. I think of her always," Tristram said with a soft nod. He sighed, with a bitter shake of his head. "Who told you of her? FitzRolf I guess?"

Ever since she had decided she would stay on as his wife, Judith had vowed to be always truthful to Tristram.

"No. Years ago... I saw the kerchief among your things."

Tristram didn't seem angry at her revelation. He raked a hand through his hair.

"I've always kept it. This kerchief she embroidered with the letter of her name, and her rosary to remember her by. She's gone to Heaven, yet even after all these years it's hard to speak her name, even in prayer."

His lady love was now dead? Judith felt wretched for having harboured such uncharitable thoughts towards a woman no longer among the living.

"Still, it is upon this day, of remembrance of her death, that I should strive to speak her name... Berenice!"

Berenice? Not Bernadette? Perchance her mother had recalled the name wrong after all. The names were similar.

"Berenice," Tristram repeated with a wistful smile upon his face. "It's only fitting that, ten years to the day she died, I should attempt to speak of my sister."

"Sister?"

The world stopped around Judith and her heart started thumping like mad. Sister?

"Twin sister, aye," Tristram amended, as if lost in a musing of his own. "My mirror image, people would say. Always attuned to me, and I to her."

He shook his head, as if recalling himself, and his voice became harsh and dispassionate.

"Enough of this though. I've had my time of prayer and remembrance. And now there are other duties to attend to."

He walked away abruptly, and Judith remained staring after him, her heart in turmoil. She'd been so wrong about this! How could she have been so wrong? And why hadn't she brought herself to ask her husband of the kerchief? Instead, she'd sought her mother's counsel. And her mother…Why would her mother speak with such knowledge of her husband's lady love? Perchance Aunt Edith had deceived her. It was no secret that Aunt Edith had wanted Judith married to her own husband's son.

Instead of feeling relief upon her husband's revelation, Judith felt guilt and grief. She'd thought Tristram in love with another, and he'd not been guilty of it. Instead, he'd been in pain, and she hadn't been able to perceive it. She went over all their remembered talks in her head, frantically, attempting to recall Tristram's gestures and words to her. His gentleness after they'd wed. His willingness to listen to her. And his genuine pleasure to talk to her. Tristram had truly listened to her and to what she'd had to say, while she… *She hadn't listened*. Because, if she had, she'd been able to understand he carried hidden grief over a most beloved sister. So he was right in his anger of her. She had betrayed him, just as he'd said she had.

As she walked down the inner bailey, caught in the turmoil of her thoughts, Judith heard a voice call her from her behind. A woman's voice.

"My lady, I am the midwife. I was told you came to look upon me some time ago, so here I am."

This was indeed the midwife in the village whom Judith had called upon some days ago on Tristram's advice. She'd not found her at home, and then she hadn't had the courage to go in seek of her again. Her name was of course familiar. She was called Nell Tyler, and when her father had been alive, she'd been his leman. Judith stared at the woman in full curiosity, because she'd often glimpsed her from afar whenever she rode to the village, but she'd never approached her or spoken to her. Judith was closely acquainted with each and every member of the villages under her care, but she had always avoided this woman. So this was Nell Tyler, the woman her father had kept. She was not beautiful, not even half as beautiful as Judith's mother. Yet Judith came to see she had keen, pretty eyes and a likeable face.

"I-I have no need of you," Judith said artlessly.

"Don't you, my lady?" Nell Tyler asked giving Judith an appraising look.

"I'm not with child, so there's naught you can help me with," Judith found herself muttering.

If the midwife had been any other woman than Nell Tyler, Judith would have brought herself to ask for her advice. But then she had resolved it had been a mistake to think her father's former mistress could ever help her in any way.

"Perchance," Nell Tyler ventured, perusing Judith with her keen eyes, "if we took a walk up the hill and talked. Your father loved that hill. I knew it always soothed him to go and think there whenever there was something he worried over."

Judith cast Nell Tyler an uneasy glance, but Nell didn't seem discomfited to talk about Judith's father.

"I–" Judith tried to think upon a way to send the woman away that would not seem harsh.

"Your mother needn't know," Nell Tyler said quite calmly. "I reckon it would upset her ladyship if she knew I came to the castle, so it's best to walk away from it."

Unwittingly, Judith found herself following Nell Tyler. There was something uncanny and soothing in her voice, which was compelling. What had Tristram's cousin said at one time? That the village midwife had the look of a witch? And Tristram had rebuked him sharply.

"You are acquainted with my husband?" she asked, recalling what Tristram had said, as she and Nell were walking out of the outer bailey.

"I spoke to him only twice, but he seems a worthy lord. Your father liked him, and Edward was always a good judge of character."

Judith stopped on her tracks.

"My-my father spoke to you of Tristram?"

"Aye, during those brief weeks he came back here from London after you'd wed. He soon went back to the city, and as you know, we never saw him again."

Judith stared uneasily at the woman in front of her. Although she was a commoner, Nell had spoken her father's name, instead of calling him her lord. And she also noted she'd spoken of his passing like a woman who'd lost a beloved husband. Yet this woman had been a leman, and she and her father had broken her mother's heart.

She shook her head.

"I'm sorry, Nell. I cannot sit and talk to you. I feel pain thinking upon such things."

Nell cast her a steady glance.

"It's often painful to speak of the dead, but it comforts me to speak of Edward, and to remember the good about him while he was alive. Of course, like all men, he had his flaws, but he was a good man, and perchance there is a thing he left unsaid. He was not a man of many words, you see, yet he always spoke of you with great pride. I thought you should know that. Perhaps I should have come upon you to tell you this a while ago, but I did not want to cause the lady Fenice even more pain."

Nell paused, as if trying to find her words, then spoke at last, "There are certain things women seek from me when they come. They seek advice and help regarding an unborn child. I help them in any way I can. And I help both those who wish for children and those who don't, although the Church will tell you my words are blasphemous. You say you're not with child. Then do you wish for a child, my lady? Or do you seek for something which would prevent conceiving a child?"

They'd resumed their walking, and soon they crossed the moat bridge and headed to the hill that Judith loved. She had not known her father had shared her love for it. She had known so little of her father, and now this woman was telling her all these things and asking her these bold questions.

"How long were you my father's woman?" she decided to ask Nell bluntly, avoiding the question the midwife had so boldly asked.

Nell laughed, apparently unconcerned by Judith's words.

"I did not count the years... Ever! Besides, there was no need of it. Edward and I had always known each other. We grew up together. And if we'd not been of different stations, we would have wed. But he was a lord, and I a midwife's daughter. His parents made him wed your mother, and I made my own match. I suppose I was luckier in mine than he was in his. I grew to care for my husband, although we had but a few short years together before death took him away from me. They were good years though – and we kept faith with each other. Your father – he and your mother could not grow to care for one another. It's sometimes thus. And your father was not to blame for it!"

"How can you say that? My father broke his wedding vows. And he broke my mother's heart. She's been heartbroken and this has built a sickness within her! She now is a prisoner in her chamber, unable to leave it for fear of being hurt by the world outside!"

Nell shook her head.

"She is a prisoner of her own making. Your father did not imprison her. For years he tried to make her care for him, and he tried to care for her in return, yet she spurned him, and he came to understand he could never get her to change towards him…"

"Had he been less harsh to her, she wouldn't have spurned him!" Judith retorted, recalling the way her mother always spoke of her father's harsh treatment of her and of his ungentle, discourteous ways.

Conjuring in her mind how her father had been, she couldn't recall ever having seen him lay a harsh hand on her mother. She recalled arguments between her parents, and sad, bitter tones, and she also recalled her father's grim, set face whenever he spoke to the lady Fenice. Her father often spoke loud and impatiently, yet she couldn't remember any truly unkind words he'd ever uttered.

Nell must have become aware of Judith's dismay, because she touched her shoulder gently.

"He was not a harsh man! And your mother might think him blunt and uncouth, but he was not one who would ever mistreat a woman. Beneath his rough appearance, he was warm and caring. He didn't have a way with words, yet when he spoke, he spoke from his heart. He only broke his wedding vows when it was plain your mother would no longer have him in her bed. For long years he tried to be a good and faithful husband, but he could not be one to a wife who would have none of him!"

"Yet it was he who broke his wedding vows! While my mother was nothing but gentle and courteous to him and did her duty by him!"

But had it been so? Judith recalled the cold tones her mother always employed when she spoke to her husband, and the disdainful way with which she looked upon him. At the time, she'd thought her mother was entitled to her rancour. Still, Nell's words seemed to hold a truth Judith was beginning to see she had failed to see before.

"Was it a mother's duty to turn a child against her own father?" Nell said, as they paused at the foot of the hill.

Judith stared at her, white in the face.

"She never did that!"

Nell shook her head with a bitter smile.

"Edward was pained! He told me you'd started to run from him when you were a child, frightened at even the sound of his voice! At first he could not understand why the little girl he'd held so often before in his arms would become so fearful of him after a long trip he'd taken to London. At first he thought it was a childish fancy which would pass, but then he came to understand you would always shun him. Your mother had taught you to fear him!"

"It is not so! Father was…"

But what had her father been like? It was not as if she'd spent many moments in his company. He'd been a busy man, overseeing his estates and doing his duty by his liege, and she had on purpose avoided his company whenever he'd been at home, seeking her mother's instead. And in those rare moments she'd been in his company, they'd spoken but little. Judith recalled how he had ordered her to marry Tristram, not caring for her own thoughts upon the matter.

"Your father loved you," Nell Tyler told her, in her soothing voice. "Though perchance he didn't know how to say it. He tried to do right by you. I remember how happy he was that time he came back from London. He spoke of the love match you were to have."

"Love match?"

"Aye, love match! Isn't that what you and Lord Tristram have in truth?"

Judith started shaking her head, deciding to tell Nell Tyler it was not for her to discuss her lady's marriage. Yet Nell Tyler didn't seem to care that Judith was her lady. And she spoke far too well for a woman of her station. Judith recalled how her mother had always told her commoners were beneath their lords, always to be pitied because they were unable to learn gentle, courteous ways. And she also recalled that her father seemed more at ease among commoners than among his peers. She remembered how well he was loved by his people, and that he'd always been fair to them. And she might not have known him well, but she knew for certain, if he'd been alive, he would have told her never to look down upon others just because of their station in life. It was a lesson she'd already learnt from him.

Judith returned her eyes upon Nell Tyler, who was one of the most astute women she'd ever set eyes upon. For so long, she'd thought her an evil woman who'd kept her father away from his lawful wife. But was it so?

"I beg forgiveness," Nell said, having noticed the look of astonishment on Judith's face. "I spoke out of turn. I couldn't help it though. I recall how pleased Edward was he'd arranged the match for you. He told me your new husband was a man whom he'd already perceived you looked upon with great longing."

"He had?" Judith muttered in puzzlement.

"Aye, and he was so happy Lord Tristram was the kind of man who could see you for what you were."

"See me?"

"Those were the words Edward used. He knew you shared his shyness and that, because of it, others were sometimes slow to see how beautiful and clever you were. He had set a test for Sir Tristram, claiming at first he had but little dowry to bestow on you upon your marriage. Sir Tristram didn't even care. And when your father asked him why it was he wished to marry you, Sir Tristram confessed he didn't know how to say it in words, yet that he somehow understood it was the only thing he could think of doing. And Edward was not a man of many words, but he could recognize a man in love when he saw one."

Judith tried hard to stop the turmoil which had begun to rage in her heart. Why had her father never tried to truly talk to her?

And Tristram… It seemed impossible Tristram could have fallen in love with someone like her.

As if in echo of her thoughts, Nell Tyler said, "Your father could see your mother's unhappiness. He felt sorry to be part of it, and knew that her lot, as a woman, was harder than his, in the loveless match they'd been both forced to make. Yet he could never bring himself to forgive her for this… in his own words, for teaching his child to fear the world, for making her believe she was in some way unworthy – unworthy of others' love. I am sure he died a happy man thinking that by the match he'd arranged for you he would get to undo this harm."

Why was this day so unlike any others? And why did all those things Judith had thought she knew seem suddenly other than what they were. For a while, she walked along with Nell Tyler, up the hill which, she'd recently come to learn, her father had also loved. Had it been he who'd brought her here first in her early childhood? Judith began to understand it must have been so. Even in her childhood, her mother rarely ventured out of the castle – a prisoner in a marriage to a man she couldn't bring herself to love, and, unlike her father, unable to escape her prison. Was it why Judith had learnt so easily how to resent her father? Because she'd been able to perceive he'd set himself free from his loveless match, while her mother hadn't ever been able to do so?

When they finally reached the top of the hill, Nell Tyler spoke of other things, those things which had prompted Judith to seek her out. She was knowledgeable in her craft and she spoke well, not thinking it blasphemous to advise Judith what to do in order to prevent conceiving a child.

"I shall prepare a pouch of herbs and a pessary for you if you do not wish to soon cradle children in your arms. And I shall school you on what days it is better to abstain from bedding, though, by the looks of your lord husband, it would be a hard thing to ever abstain," Nell Tyler said with a wink and a smile.

"Why is it that you are so willing to help me?" Judith asked in sheer wonder, recalling she'd spurned this woman and had never even deigned to speak to her.

"You're Edward's daughter," Nell Tyler said in her steady, soothing voice.

"Am I so like him? My mother always said…"

"You are like both your parents, and yet in some ways unlike them. All children are so. But I am certain you know this already, don't you, my lady?" the midwife said as they looked upon the green hills.

CHAPTER 21

*T*ristram winced slightly as he pulled his tunic over his head. He'd come to the bedchamber to change his garments, seeking a time when Judith was not there. It was best he didn't look upon her or share a chamber. Because if he did, he would be sorely tempted to let go of all his anger towards her and treat her gently. Yet she'd deceived him before, had broken his heart before, and he did not want his heart broken again by her.

Fetching the jar of salve he still had left, and promising to soon seek Nell Tyler out to collect more of the medicine, he attempted to nurse his sore back as well as he could. The whip scars may have had a better chance of healing had he not received the penance to wear a hair shirt every Friday until Lent. They'd flogged him in Church not a month past, a flogging he'd chosen to take upon himself in order to spare his wife from the punishment that had been bestowed upon her for standing against him. He'd reasoned with them he was the one to blame for his lady's transgressions, having been unable to school her to due obedience. As such, the fault lay with him for not guiding her. The punishment Judith should have had would have been a flogging after they'd shorn her hair and paraded her in Church for all to see what happens to treacherous, defiant wives. Yet Tristram would not have it. He would not let them hurt and belittle the one he loved.

Tristram's family had been angered by his obstinacy to shield a woman who'd humiliated their noble house. They had prevailed upon Henry and the Church to request a solemn vow from Tristram that, should he keep his treacherous wife, he would make this defiant woman repent and rue the day of her betrayal. Tristram had made the vow, right before the flogging, that he would from now on keep his wife repentant and chastised. Still, those prelates who had looked upon him making the vow had caught the look of stubborn pride in his eyes when he had spoken the words. Pride was a grievous sin. They had bestowed further penance on him after the flogging. A hair shirt would cure him of his prideful ways and help him see he'd been wrong to indulge a woman who'd defied him.

In this, King Henry had cared but very little for how his vassal chose to make a fool of himself over a woman. If Tristram chose to take a flogging himself, instead of having his wife flogged, so be it then, as long as the Church and Tristram's family were appeased. As long as Tristram made sure his wife would never step out of bounds again or seek a new treacherous cause, Henry didn't so much care for what happened to Lady Judith. Redmore was his concern, and once Tristram held Redmore, all would be well. A secure stronghold and the due chastisement of a rebellious wife was all Henry asked for, and Tristram had clung to that, gritting his teeth against the pain and humiliation of the flogging he'd borne.

He shook his head to himself recalling that day, and the gleeful, malicious faces of all those who'd witnessed his punishment, and who'd revelled callously in seeing a lord of high blood so humbled. In spite of it all, Tristram knew he could never have done otherwise, and that he'd do it a thousand times over to keep Judith from harm. He had resolved they would never touch her. And it was a vow he would never break.

He now tried to spread what he had left of Nell Tyler's salve on his back as well as he could, cursing his own pride and knowing he should have had one of his squires attend to him.

"Tristram!"

He winced. His back was turned on the door and he'd been busy at his task, with his mind on his troubles. It had been hard to sense that Judith had entered the chamber. He suppressed a deep sigh, fully aware that now she could see his back, and the whip scars whose full healing the hair shirt had deferred. Judith's voice was deeply anguished, and a treacherous part of Tristram's soul rejoiced in her anguish. Yet he had meant to hide the scars from her. He did not want her gratitude. He'd always wanted her love. But he'd come to see it was something it was most likely she could never give him.

"What's this? Who did this to you?" Judith asked in the same high, anguished voice.

Tristram sighed deeply.

"Instead of prattling, perchance you could come and help nurse my back since you're already here."

He closed his eyes as soon as Judith came to tend to him, immersing himself in the bliss of having her soft fingers spread the salve in order to soothe his skin.

"You're hurt!" Judith said in the same voice which seemed anguished.

"Don't make so much of it," Tristram growled, now already beginning to feel vexed with the way she was behaving. "It hardly pains me. And in a few weeks' time I shall be rid of the accursed penance shirt, so I'll be the better for it."

"But why? Who'd whip a lord? And why the penance?"

Tristram found he'd had enough of his wife's care. He pushed her hand aside and fetched the fresh tunic he'd prepared.

"It was all for my sins," he said tersely, knowing it was best she never learnt of it.

He did not want Judith's gratitude, and had never sought it. What he had done had been because he'd wanted it so.

"Sins? What sins were those?" Judith now asked, not letting him be.

"They're mine. I do not care to share them."

Tristram strode to the door, knowing he needed to go away from her at this time. Yet Judith called after him, and this made him stop in his tracks.

"It was for my sake, wasn't it? So that *they* wouldn't chastise me!"

He closed his eyes wearily.

"Just look at me! Say something!" Judith pleaded.

Tristram would have wanted to say many things to his wife, but at this time he resolved it was best not to speak to her. Nothing good would come of it. He would be again tempted to think there might be hope she cared for him somewhat, even in spite of the wretched way in which she'd spurned him.

JUDITH REMAINED STARING AFTER TRISTRAM, deeply shaken by what she'd perceived. Her shame burnt fiercely, because she at last understood that Tristram had not only thought to shield her in this but he'd suffered for her sake, with no regard for himself. They'd hurt him. She pictured the scene in her head as tears welled in her eyes. They'd hurt her beautiful Tristram. And she herself had been the cause of it. In truth, she'd been the one to hurt him.

For hours on end she was numb, unable to think. At last, she began to feel torn between grief and joy. Because she finally understood that Tristram's words all those years ago had been true. He loved her. Truly loved her. Immeasurably so it seemed, because he'd borne pain and humiliation for her, even if she had spurned him. She'd been so blind and wicked – unable to see that the words she'd feared so much were true.

When at last her mother called for her, Judith went to see her in the solar, shaking her head to herself and understanding how blind she'd been. She stared at her mother, now at last beginning to see her for what she was in truth – a woman who was deeply sick, and whose counsel she had trusted when she should have relied only upon herself. All those years ago, Tristram had been right to tell her she'd been a child. And today was perchance the first day in which she was a child no longer.

"At last I've had an answer from my sister, to the letter I sent her," Lady Fenice said, perusing a piece of parchment and, for once, unable to see her daughter's distress.

"Oh," Judith said, having recently learned from Lord FitzRolf that the lady Edith might be forced to take the veil and join a priory.

Lady Fenice then went on, telling the tale of how King Henry hadn't been inclined to entirely forgive her aunt for her ardent support for Queen Eleanor's cause. Yet he'd chosen to be lenient on his foes, since he knew many of them still held powerful connections in France. As Lady Edith's own husband had been killed in the rebellion some months ago, the king had taken possession of the rebel's fortune, leaving the lady Edith with only enough to join the convent.

"What of Raymond?" Judith asked, because she had always been fond of her young step-cousin.

"He managed to escape to France, and he sought to join our kin in Aquitaine. Yet he didn't receive the warm welcome he'd expected."

"At least he's safe from Henry's wrath!" Judith mused with relief.

King Henry might have been lenient on most of those who'd played a part in the rebellion, but some of his punishments had been swift – those he'd bestowed upon the noble lords and ladies who'd played a portentous part in the rebellion. So it was a relief that Judith's cousin had escaped with his life. He had a chance of building a new life for himself in France, and maybe, in time, Henry would be even brought to pardon him for his parents' deeds and rescind his exile.

"My brother," Lady Fenice said in sheer anguish, "is not the man I thought he was! It seems he wishes to have none of us or our kin!"

The news did not surprise Judith. For years, she'd begun to suspect her Occitan uncle had grown sour towards his sisters who resided on English soil. She could not begin to guess the cause of this enmity, but it was plain there was no place for her mother in her brother's home.

"We have a home here," she said gently.

She stared upon her mother, knowing already what she'd been too blind to see all these years. Her mother was indeed sick, but she was more diseased than even Judith had imagined. Her unhappiness had loomed like a large dark shadow upon her and Judith's lives. Nell Tyler was right. In some ways, her mother was a prisoner of her own making.

"A home," Lady Fenice scoffed. "At the fiend's mercy?"

"Hush, Mother, Tristram is no fiend," Judith said wearily.

She thought of Tristram, and of how Tristram had attempted to protect her even when she'd spurned him and had judged him unfairly. Of how Tristram had borne the pain and the humiliation of a flogging for her sake. She had misjudged her husband grievously. And she could not blame her own blindness fully on her mother. She herself was to blame for the troubles in her marriage.

"Oh, I see now," her mother said and her voice rang ugly and full of venom, unlike her usually melodious tones. "He's enslaved you with his bedchamber eyes and sinful ways. How many times have I told you men are not to be trusted? Are you so shallow that you only think of the ways of the flesh? That you allow him to rule you just because you can't get enough of his lechery?"

Judith stood silent, gazing through the window at the world outside which her mother had pushed away.

"I see how it is. You are his puppet now in every way! I knew this would happen ever since my sister first wrote about the lovesick way you gazed upon him at Court. I urged then for the match with Raymond, yet your dull father would have none of it!" Lady Fenice ranted.

Judith turned, feeling deep heat rise in her cheeks.

"You and Edith! You always plotted to have me parted from Tristram, I see that now. And as for Edith, I can see why she wished for her stepson to have my dowry. But you... You always knew I was in love with Tristram. Why were you so set against him?"

"I thought to spare you the heartache! A man like him would have never kept faith with a woman like you!"

"Why? Because he is accomplished in every way and because you see me as dim-witted and ugly? Because you see me as unworthy of a good man's love?"

The words rang bitter, in echo of what Nell Tyler had uttered. *He wants to marry you, daughter.* Her own father's words at the time he'd urged for her match with Tristram. She hadn't understood at the time what her father had meant, but it was now as clear as day that in his own artless way her father had been trying to convey to her that Tristram could learn to love her for herself, not for the dowry she would bring. And Tristram did love her, in spite of the wretched way she'd behaved to him.

"It is not so, my sweet one!" Lady Fenice uttered, taken aback by Judith's forceful words. "He's broken your heart already, and he will break it, again and again! It's all a game to him, just as I've often said!"

Judith shook her head with a hollow laugh.

"You truly believe he can't ever love me for myself. And

you've made *me* believe it. You even stooped to lie about his lady love at Court!"

Lady Fenice's face went crimson.

"You are mistaken. I don't recall ever telling for certain he had a lady love. And even if I did, it was my sister Edith's own words that I was repeating!"

"Did Edith ever see him with this lady?"

"It is what she said! I was only repeating her words."

Lady Fenice's tone was gentle and sweet, and, perchance another time, Judith would have strived to believe her mother spoke the truth, yet this day had been a day of revelations. And Judith had grown sick of deceiving herself.

"Nay. You lied! I wonder even if there's a lady by that name. Perchance she's all a lie you conjured up. A heinous lie! And I was foolish enough to believe you. What of the letter telling me the Church had annulled my marriage to Tristram? I showed it to Tristram's cousin, and he pointed out the seal was but a clever look-alike. Was that still Edith? Let me guess… Not only she, but you and she, in league. What did you think to accomplish by leading me to believe my marriage was over? Make it appear I stood against Tristram so that he may forever forsake me?"

"I…"

Lady Fenice suddenly clutched her chest.

"My heart… I do not feel well. Why are you saying such cruel, unfeeling things to make me ill? Accusing me of lying?"

Judith closed her eyes briefly, then called upon a servant to tend to Lady Fenice by giving her a restorative potion. She understood her mother genuinely believed herself ill in her body, although the illness resided only in her soul. It was an illness that had caused her to disregard her own daughter's wishes or happiness. And Judith saw her mother still fervently believed she had been doing this for Judith's welfare and protection. And for this, she'd stooped to lying and treachery.

"Forgive me, Mother," she said, now striving to speak gently, perceiving her mother's sickness was a powerful one and that Lady Fenice may never see the error of her ways. "I did not mean to make you ill."

Lady Fenice nodded with a tremulous smile, now obediently drinking the potion the servant had handed her. It was in truth a restorative tea made of cat's valerian which the physician had recommended. He'd told Judith it had no healing power, but just a mild calming effect. However, while she'd been told what it was, Lady Fenice was persuaded it was a good medicine for her ailing heart.

"Yet I did not tell you what Edith further said," her mother went on, when it seemed she was feeling better.

Judith strived to keep her composure and to listen calmly to what her mother had to say.

"Edith spoke of Severborough Priory as a place of peace and tranquillity. A place of contemplation. With pleasant gardens, and a prioress of noble blood who's mindful of those who are of high birth. Edith herself is content there, and she tells me of books and songs and even of other entertainments which can be had. There are several women of our station in that place of solace, who were forced to take the veil or reside there, like-minded souls who supported our queen's cause. It got me thinking. As our own home seems lost to us forever, you and I could go to this place where we'd be free of men and their harsh ways!"

"Free? This is a convent, Mother! No matter what Aunt Edith says, convent life is bound by harsh rules!"

Her mother waved her hand. "I never told you, but at one time I thought to join a convent. Convent life seemed a far better prospect than being married to your father."

"Was Father truly so harsh and unkind to you, Mother?" Judith couldn't help asking now, hoping her mother would not become newly distressed by her question.

Lady Fenice shrugged, apparently unbothered by her daughter's boldness.

"He was a man I could not ever care for, with his uncouth and savage ways. A fiend, just like your husband is, but in a different way. Your lord is clever and well-spoken, but underneath all this he's only savage – just as savage and as fiendish as your father was."

Her mother stared intently away from Judith, as if not seeing her, and enwrapped in thoughts of her own.

"So we shall leave as soon as can be, away from here! To the safe haven this convent is!" she said, with deep feeling.

"You'll have me seek a convent?" Judith asked in full wonder.

"Certainly. It is the best thing for you, and you'll come to see I'm right. At one time, when you were very young, I even spoke of it to your father, and he just bellowed at me in anger. I was wrong to bend to his will at the time. Marriage is not for you. I raised you to be gentle and caring."

Judith simply stared at her mother, who was now completely wrapped up in her thoughts of keeping her daughter from the world outside. And she closed her eyes in sheer weariness, because she finally understood all she'd failed to see for all these years. Her mother did not truly see her. She never had. She only saw her own desires and plans of happiness, uncaring her daughter loved the man she'd married, uncaring of Judith's own wishes and dreams, and thinking them misguided and unworthy. Yet, Judith also understood, in her own way, just like her father, her mother loved her and wanted what she thought best for her. It was only that her mother couldn't ever understand that what she wanted wasn't what was best for Judith.

"Redmore is the best place for me. And marriage is the best thing for me, Mother. I love my home. And I love Tristram. I've come to see that Tristram loves me. And from now on I shall strive to think myself worthy of his love. This is my home, and it cannot be otherwise!" she spoke the words gently, kissing her mother's forehead.

Lady Fenice pushed her away, and tears of rage soon started to fall upon her cheeks.

"He's turned you against me, the fiend! I can see now you believe the lies he's weaved. Oh, Edith was right all along! She told me you might never wish to leave this place. Yet *I* will!"

Judith tried to plead with her mother, but it seemed that at this time the lady Fenice had become too distraught to speak, and Judith understood it was to no avail to attempt to reason with her. She left the solar, telling herself she would resume the talk and make her mother understand this place would always be better than a priory.

CHAPTER 22

J udith did not set eyes upon her husband for the rest
of the day, yet she resolved her course was set. She
had erred grievously towards him, and she now
vowed to herself to seek his forgiveness and never to pass wrong
judgement upon him again. Her grief over the hurt she'd caused
was mixed with the joy she was loved in return. Tristram did
love her, and this meant there was the shadow of a hope things
could be mended between them, once she told him of her love
and remorse.

Still, she simply stirred in pain to think of what Tristram had
endured for her sake. Not only had he borne a painful, humiliating flogging which, she now fully understood, had been meant
for her, he also had received the penance of the hair shirt she'd
seen him wear this Friday. Judith now understood this penance
must also be for her sake. And she started asking herself whether
she should tell Tristram that *she* would gladly wear it from now
on. Still – her whole being revolted against the thing when she
sought it out in Tristram's garment chest. In her eyes, it was an
ugly, vicious thing which had tormented her Tristram, and no

matter how guilty she felt towards her husband, this ugly thing had no place in their lives from now on.

Resolutely, with a servant's help, she busied herself to kindle a fire in the hearth. The servant looked at her askance, because it was August, but he assisted his mistress with what was required of him. When she'd thanked and dismissed the servant, Judith simply proceeded to throw the penance shirt into the fire, her nostrils filling with the pungent smell of it as soon as it started to burn. She looked at it for a while in grim satisfaction, not stirring when she heard the door and footsteps behind her. When she turned, Tristram was staring at her with a hard expression on his beautiful face.

"I thought you were gone from the chamber," he said tersely, and turned to leave.

"Wait!" Judith cried, pulling her shoulders back. "The penance shirt..."

Her words stopped Tristram in his tracks, but he didn't turn to look at her.

"I burnt it," Judith said striving to keep her voice level.

Tight-lipped and pale, Tristram returned to stare at the hearth and at the burnt remains of the instrument of his penance. When he turned to look upon Judith, his dark eyes were pitch-black against the white skin of his face.

"If you think you can make me foresworn, you are mistaken. I always keep vows. You burnt this one, I'll have another made," he said in a voice which was utterly cold.

Judith held herself straight, staring at him without flinching.

"I do not care at all for the vow you must have made in front of men who mean nothing to me," she said laying emphasis on every word she uttered. "God is wise, and does not wish for people to suffer unjustly. The penance is unjust, and it stops now. If there's someone who deserves a penance for what happened between us, I am the one. I take it fully upon myself. And it's only upon you to bestow it on me."

"I will chastise you for this. But then I'll keep my vow," Tristram said in the same cold voice.

"Fine. And I will burn the next penance shirt you mean to wear. And then the next," Judith said with a shrug. "Chastise me all you wish!"

"You're saying so now, but we shall see," he countered.

"If you are looking for the birch, it still lies in the corner where you last tossed it," Judith told him, feeling light-hearted and unconcerned.

She would bear his anger and whatever punishment he resolved she deserved for having doubted his love. Yet she would never bear that he should suffer for her sake ever again. Still, there were things which needed to be said before she accepted her punishment.

"BEFORE YOU CHASTISE ME, I need to say true words it's best to utter before the punishment," Judith said and her voice sounded firm and self-assured.

Tristram tried to still his laboured breathing, understanding Judith now meant to stir his anger. He clenched his fists, knowing too well the next words his wife would utter would still be words of sheer defiance. However, it was not words of defiance that Judith spoke to him now.

"I beg forgiveness. And I'm not doing so in order to escape your punishment. In fact, I welcome whatever you wish to bestow upon me."

She bowed her head humbly, and although Tristram had kept telling himself he would rejoice in seeing Judith truly humbled, it made him uneasy to think he was the one who'd brought her to this state. She kept her eyes downcast for a long while, her body still, her hands clasped and her head still lowered in humility in front of him.

"Look at me, wife!" he ended up telling her artlessly, not knowing what else to say.

He would always love her. And no matter how hard he'd tried to tell himself he no longer cared for her, the truth was different. She would always have his heart, however little she actually cared for him – that was a thing not even God above could change.

"Forgive me, husband!" Judith now entreated him, and her melodious voice sounded so heart-breaking that Tristram simply wanted to weep.

He'd fancied hearing the words so many times before, because he'd been so angry with her for how she'd behaved. Yet once she'd spoken the words, he found he was the one who was supposed to ask for her forgiveness. He'd been harsh to her and ungentle. Through his disdain, he'd sought to punish her for spurning his love, but she was not to blame for not loving him. He was the one to blame for loving her and for clinging so stubbornly to that love.

"Hush," he muttered. "These are not words I wish to hear from your lips."

"I see. It's different words you want to hear, and I know now what they are. I should have spoken them sooner. Far sooner than this! I love you."

He turned his gaze away from her, hating the way his heart started to thump like mad when she uttered the words he'd always craved to hear. And then he stared at her, unable to look away. The way she'd spoken the words in the voice he would never have enough of hearing... they rang true. Did they ring true only because he wished them to be true?

"I love you," Judith repeated in a steady voice. "For so long I believed myself unworthy of your love. So I made myself unworthy of it. And this is how I behaved. I doubted you. I was afraid to tell you of my love, and I was too blind to see what plainly lay in front of me. But if you think I can make myself worthy of your love again, then I…"

Tristram closed the distance between them in two quick strides. He took his wife in his arms and kissed her passionately. And he spoke against her lips urgently.

"You're never to say such things again!"

"What? You do not ever want me to say I love you?" Judith muttered as she languidly pressed herself against him.

He gave a rueful laugh.

"Nay! Not that. That you can tell me as often as you wish. Those other things you said… It is I who need to beg your forgiveness. I truly thought you didn't love me at all. I was so angry over it. And harsh. And ungentle…"

Judith shook her head, and her hand came to cup his cheek.

"Harsh perhaps, but never ungentle," she said, bestowing an ardent kiss upon his lips.

Their loving afterwards was very sweet, and Tristram found himself recalling all those times he'd spanked her hard. He had been ungentle to Judith, no matter what she said. At the time, he'd told himself the spankings meant to ensure her obedience were the only way to make his cousin and those around them believe his wife had been well and duly chastened. Still, he had revelled in those punishments. It was a thing he needed to confess to her.

"I *was* ungentle. I spanked you hard and made you sob in pain. And I rejoiced in it," he told her, knowing they would have to be entirely truthful to one another. "I took pleasure in all those times I chastened you."

Yet, as he said that, he couldn't help but recall Judith's own soaking quim after the punishments, and the sounds of rapture which had been mingled with sobs and tears. As if in echo of his thoughts, Judith now muttered, "And *I* also took pleasure in those…"

Tristram shook his head in some wonder, and then burst into unrestrained laughter.

"And at first I thought I would be doing such a good job of duly punishing you."

"But you did," she retorted.

"Oh, did I?" Tristram purred in turn.

"You know you did," Judith answered with a smile.

She cupped his face, now looking intently into his eyes.

"And you can still punish me all you wish. Yet there'll be no more hair shirts in this household. I meant it when I said I'd burn each and every one of them."

He scowled at her.

"I swore an oath before God," he said, now looking grim.

"Their God. Your cousin's God of hatred. Not mine or yours," Judith said quietly. "You know too well I'm right."

He closed his eyes, knowing indeed men of his cousin's ilk would think Judith's words heresy. Still, he knew deep within himself that she had the right of it. He felt free of the penance. To him, it had been in truth a penance he'd upheld in order to punish himself for the love he'd lost. Yet now that love had been regained.

"Fine. No more hair shirts," he found himself muttering.

Judith beamed at him and he cocked an eyebrow at her. Now, unlike other times, they found themselves in agreement, and he was no longer used to being in agreement with his wife.

"I begin to be half sorry we're reconciled. Now it will be hard to find excuses to chastise you," he told her with a smile which was half wicked and half wistful.

"You still love games, don't you?" Judith countered, with a faint smile on her lips. "Don't tell me you don't. You always have!"

"So, wife, you're saying you will wish to play that game with me? The game of chastisement?"

"I am!"

"Yet there will be not only pleasure, but also pain for you in it. I do not think I'll be able to help spanking you hard. It may be sinful of me, but I've come to take delight in it,"

"Both pain and pleasure mingled," Judith mused. "Isn't that what life always is? Both pain and pleasure?"

"At times," Tristram nodded.

"Then we should play the game at times," Judith nodded in her turn. "Strange as it is, it is a game we have both come to enjoy. It is, after all, a game of love."

Tristram smiled faintly, understanding she was right. It was a strange game. Yet love was strange at times.

"I suppose I knew I loved you from the first moment I heard your voice," he said. "It is a strange thing indeed. Like the love philtre which compelled Tristan to love his Yseult. Something I simply felt from the start and could not ever help. But I suspect you didn't love me from the start. Perhaps it was my own fault for not courting you properly. You were too young, and had not had time to get accustomed to things other than your home. And then misfortunes happened which prevented us from being with one another, and when at last we were together again, I found you pushing me away. Was it because you didn't love me at the time that you sought to annul our marriage?" he asked.

JUDITH HAD PROMISED to be entirely truthful to her husband.

"I was in love with you from the first. Like a fanciful child. But I suppose that being in love is not the same thing as loving. I really learned to love you as time went by. And, in truth, I sought to annul our bond out of misguided jealousy. I thought you loved another. I simply couldn't bear it and I didn't even seek to ask you if there was true cause for my jealousy."

Tristram sat up and looked at her in sheer puzzlement.

"Why would you ever think I loved another? I have always

been true to you! Even during the year we were estranged. Even when I tried to think upon other women, I could not help it. I could not help always keeping faith with you!"

Judith felt even more wretched for having mistrusted her husband so. She now vowed she would make things up to him, and be forever the best of wives.

"It was wrong of me to misjudge you without giving you a chance to defend yourself. And we both know it is a grievous error you should chastise me for."

She laced both repentance and teasing in her voice.

"And let us not forget you did burn my penance shirt. In full defiance," Tristram added.

He grinned at her broadly as he uttered the words, yet he didn't tarry to place her over his lap.

"It is a good thing you're already naked, though this does rob me of the pleasure of hoisting your skirts and baring your bottom."

He spanked her bottom lightly for a while, until Judith felt a pleasant heat all through her body. It was sheer bliss when he began to tend to her quim, just as she lay on his lap. It didn't take much tending for her sex to clench and pulse in rapture. And she did so, and at the very time of her fierce climax, Tristram began to spank her again, harder than before. It was heated bliss, Judith mused later as she later lay upon her belly, spent and sated, and she had to confess that never had a punishment from him seemed more delicious. Tristram watched her through hooded dark eyes.

"So, wife, you've had your bliss. Now it's my turn."

"Certainly, my lord," Judith purred, positioning herself for what she knew would be a good thrust of his already eager cock.

She lifted her bottom at him, setting herself on her elbows and knees, because she well recalled he'd liked to have her this way.

"Stay as you are," Tristram called to her, yet he strode away from the bed.

Judith frowned in puzzlement, looking at him over her shoulder. What did he mean to do? She blanched, because she now perceived Tristram had presently returned to their bed, carrying in his hand the birch which had lain forgotten in its corner.

"Tristram…" she muttered in alarm.

"Did I say you can look upon me?" Tristram countered in return and his voice was a mixture of both playful and stern.

"Nay, but…"

"Stay as you were. And stop prattling," he commanded, and Judith heaved a heartfelt sigh, but complied with what he'd told her.

"You did ask for the birch earlier, didn't you?" Tristram said, now speaking softly, and beginning to caress the reddened skin of Judith's buttocks with the birch.

It was a tantalizing sensation, and Judith's heart began to thump wildly. The birch caressed her skin and she recalled only too well its fierce sting as she'd stood facing the wall after she'd been soundly punished. Did Tristram mean only to tease her with it? Or did he mean to punish her soundly? Judith did not have time to answer the question because Tristram began to birch her bottom lightly. The birching was indeed light, yet soon Judith began to feel that a fiercer sting was building there.

"Tristram," she said rather plaintively, and Tristram paused, and spoke to her in a lazy voice.

"Your behind is already somewhat striped from the birch. Faint, reddish stripes all over your plump buttocks and thighs."

His talk already kindled a fire between Judith's legs and she found herself thrusting her bottom further towards him, hoping he would soon enter her and sate her maddening lust.

"So eager for my punishment, wife…"

Now Tristram birched her bottom hard, making Judith arch

her back in sheer surprise and pain, as a stab of deep pleasure coursed through her.

"Oh, husband, it stings so," she complained in both pain and rapture.

Soon she had cause to smile, because she heard Tristram simply tossing away the birch and had occasion to feel him thrust deep inside her, loving her hard and savagely, with one of his hands buried into her long dark hair. However, Tristram didn't seem to sate his lust for chastisement, not even after they were both done and spent. Instead, he put her again over his knee for a new spanking which stung even worse, because her bottom was already red and tender, both from his birching and from the way he'd loved her from behind.

His spanking left her rubbing her bottom and softly crying, and Tristram took great pleasure in licking the salty tears off her face, telling her afterwards he'd never thought tears could taste so sweet.

"I am beginning to think I erred when I promised to play the game of chastisement with you," Judith said at last with a frown. She couldn't help but add a half-smile to the frown. "You are a strange man, husband, after all. So gentle and so harsh at the same time."

Yet she truly began to fear Tristram would spank her anew, when at last she told him the full story of her misguided jealousy over the tokens she'd found in his trunk. Tristram did threaten to spank her sore, with his sword belt, if she ever doubted him like that ever again, but he held her in a warm embrace just as he was making his threat. Judith suppressed a smile, knowing already she would get to feel that belt upon her behind, in their bed, even if she didn't cross her husband ever again.

"The flower – was that another thing to remember your dear sister by?" she asked, as she was idly stroking Tristram's fair hair.

At first he widened his eyes in puzzlement, but then he shook his head with a smile. Judith's eyes roamed over his beautiful nakedness as he strode to his garment chest. She sighed, under-standing some of the scars left by the whip he'd endured for her sake might become lasting marks upon his back even once it was fully healed. Certainly, the scars would never deter from his beauty in her eyes, yet she felt guilty to have been the cause of them.

"Is this the flower you found?" Tristram said, coming to sit by her, holding the dry pressed flower in his hand.

Judith nodded, blushing with shame for the way she'd misjudged him. She'd thought the flower a love token from another woman. Yet it was not so.

"It is a love token indeed," he said, coming to cup her face. "But it is not one I keep in remembrance of my sister. In truth, I keep it in remembrance of you."

Judith widened her eyes.

"Of me?"

"You do recall I told you I fell in love with you when I first heard your voice."

"Aye, I recall when we first met. You were blindfolded."

"Yet it was not the first time I had heard your voice. The first time – I heard it in the garden. You were gone when I got there, but there was a sweetbriar on that spot."

Now Judith remembered one blissful morning she'd spent in the gardens at Court singing by a sweetbriar. She shook her head in wonder.

"Why did you never tell me of it? I wish you had! Then I'd have been able to perceive your true love for me!"

She paused, staring sadly at the love token and feeling deep regret at all the years they'd lost because they'd failed to confess their love for each other. Tristram heaved a sigh, kissing the top of her head.

"I suppose it was my own silly pride. I did not even want to own up to myself I'd tumbled in love with a woman just at the sound of her voice. Yet it was what it was. I see now though that what you say is true. I fell in love with you then, like a fanciful child, but it was only after I got to know you that I learnt to love you in truth. And when we reunited, I learnt to love you anew."

"That is a fine tale of courtly love, the way you speak of it. You've always enjoyed such tales, my lord Tristram."

"And so have you, my lady Judith," Tristram countered. "Perchance you could make one of your songs of it."

"A song," Judith mused. "No. A tale is better. It seems better to have a tale of this, yet it would be a mightily strange tale. I don't know if such a story has ever been written... in Norman or in Occitan..."

"Make it in English then," Tristram suddenly said.

Judith frowned. English? Who'd ever heard of courtly tales written on parchment in English? They called such tales *romanz*, and French was the language of them. Yet now she thought better on it, Tristram had the right of it. Somehow, when she conjured up the words to tell it, she understood their strange tale of love lost and regained would sound even better in English than in Norman or Occitan.

"Whose English? My English?" she said, unable not to tease him, although he'd learnt to speak the English of the North quite well.

"Yours, to be sure," he said with a teasing smile of his own. "It seems a more fitting means to tell of the ways in which I chastised you."

She frowned.

"If I ever bring myself to put on parchment such a tale, I mean to leave the chastisements aside from it. It is a tale of courtly love, after all!"

"I don't see anything wrong with a *romanz* telling of chastisements or of heated love," Tristram shrugged.

"Truly? And what do you think the Church would say of it?" Judith asked with a cocked eyebrow.

Tristram waved his hand.

"They'd probably mean to punish us for the blasphemous sinners we are," he said, yet his voice sounded light and unconcerned as he spoke the words.

Judith found herself brushing her fingers upon his scarred back, then beginning to kiss each of the scars her husband had borne for her.

"Don't ever speak so lightly of it," she said between kisses. "They hurt you. And you let yourself hurt for my sake."

He cast her a brilliant, careless smile, and spoke to her in a steady voice.

"Yet for your sake I'd do it a thousand times over. It is just as it is."

But Judith placed a staying finger on his lips.

"Nay. Never again! I will not let them hurt you. And perchance it's best certain courtly tales are left unwritten. I'd rather have my husband safe and sound rather than a knight who suffers for my sake."

Tristram's lips kissed her fingers.

"Fine then. Have it your own way, although the Church need never learn of it even if you write a *romanz* that tells of heated love. Besides, they would simply dismiss it if it were written in English."

"I was not speaking of the *romanz* or of what the Church may or may not do about it. I was speaking of *your deeds*, Tristram. I need your vow you will never again put yourself in any peril for my sake!"

"You know well it is a vow I cannot ever make or keep," Tristram told her steadily.

Judith sighed deeply, because she'd come to know her husband. He was and would always be not only her husband but also a knight, who felt bound to protect her at all costs.

"Fine then, *I* shall make you a vow. One I'd rather die than ever break. I vow to also protect *you* at all costs," she said, suddenly brightening and knowing that from now on she would strive to do everything in her power to prevent her beloved Tristram from coming to any harm.

He scowled at her.

"That is not a vow a lady should ever make to her lord!"

"Why ever not?" Judith countered with an arched eyebrow.

"Because it is *my* duty to protect you!"

"Mine also, from now on. I shall protect you in return," Judith countered, content she'd found the right way of it and knowing she would forever keep this vow.

Tristram looked downright flustered for a moment. He however began to smile after a while, and cocked an eyebrow at her, telling her in a teasing voice, "In truth, *your* duty is to mind whatever *I* say, my lady. And be soundly spanked if you do not."

Judith rolled her eyes at her husband, knowing full well this might earn her a new spanking from him.

"My bottom's sore already!" she complained, however letting Tristram hear that her complaint was half feigned.

"Not sore enough, since you still dare to roll your eyes at me," Tristram countered with a wicked grin on his lips.

"A heartless man you are!" Judith tossed at him, not resisting to goad him even further and already feeling her heart thump in anticipation at the further game they were going to play.

CHAPTER 23

*T*he next day seemed like the most wonderful day in
Judith's life, although the sky was grey and cloudy. Yet
her happiness was soon disturbed when the serving women
brought Judith the news that Lady Fenice was no longer in her
chambers. It soon turned out that Judith's mother had indeed
left the castle, in secrecy, with only a couple of retainers to
accompany her. Judith's heart simply skipped with fear because
she was aware her mother had not left her chambers in several
years. And it was perchance more than ten years since Lady
Fenice had stepped out of the castle.

"She went in the night. In secrecy!" Judith wrung her hands
in distress. "What if something happens to her? She's not known
the world outside in so long. I do so fear for her!"

Tristram put his arm around her shoulders.

"Do you know where she might have gone?" he asked.

Judith nodded, recalling only too well her mother's wish to
be with her sister, and she told Tristram of the letter her mother
had received.

"We shall send word to Severborough at once. Let us hope

she will reach it safely," Tristram said, before striding to call upon one of his men.

It was with sheer relief that, several days later, Judith received the news her mother had indeed reached the priory, and the men Tristram had sent to make inquiries returned with a letter which bore Lady Fenice's seal. It was a short letter, which plainly stated that Judith's mother was at present happy where she was and had no further wish to return upon the dark home which had been her prison for so many years.

"I did not know your mother was so unhappy here," Tristram mused when Judith let him read the letter. "I knew she was ailing, but I always assumed it was only due to her frail health. Perchance Severborough may indeed prove a place of solace to her!"

"It is a convent! How can anyone find any measure of solace in such a place?" Judith asked with an anguished shake of her head.

Tristram shook his head.

"Some people do. Those who have a calling for that kind of life. And you're wrong to think this priory a bleak place. As you know, a large part of my family is in the Church. My second cousin is now prioress there. She joined the priory by her own choice and she concerns herself with the welfare of those who reside there. She's always told me she seeks to make Severborough into a safe haven for women who wish to spend their time away from this world. You would certainly not be suited for convent life, but you are wrong to think your mother may be so unhappy there. It seems to me she's already put aside the world outside."

Tristram's words were meant to be soothing, and it was true her mother had long parted from the world outside the walls of her chamber. Yet Judith had to see for herself. So Tristram accompanied her to Severborough. It was a three-day journey, but not arduous. Nevertheless Judith wondered how it was that her mother, so used to spending time only in her chambers, had managed to make this trip. At last, they came upon the priory, and soon Judith had occasion to see that Tristram's cousin was a kindly woman, who welcomed them with a serene smile upon her face. The pleasant gardens and the content faces of the women there, some dressed in nun's garb, yet others in lay clothes, made Judith breathe a sigh of sheer relief. However, the solace she felt upon perceiving this was not a bleak place was soon disturbed when she set eyes on her aunt Edith. Unlike the faces of the other women here, Edith's face was pinched and full of malice.

Tristram's cousin had already told Judith her mother was presently in her cell and was ready to welcome her. However Edith seemed to have already learnt Judith was on her way to see Lady Fenice.

"So," Judith's aunt said, drawing her aside, "I hear Lord Tristram has decided to keep you on as his wife. Word goes he even took a flogging for *your* sake," she went on in mocking tones.

Judith pretended not to hear her.

"How fares Raymond? I hope he's safe and sound!" she said, because she was indeed fond of her step-cousin, who was a mild, kindly boy.

"As well as can be expected. He lives. And I suppose he should be thankful for that. Yet he's not as fortunate as some," Edith said, looking pointedly at Judith.

Then she added, in a voice which seeped with venom, "I always told my sister not to disparage your ill looks or lack of wit. God saw fit to endow you with the body and ways of a slattern, and surely even a man unable to claim his husbandly rights is lured by such easy charms. And now these charms served you well indeed. You've both a husband and a home."

Judith had meant to feel sorry for her aunt, whose husband had fallen in battle and who'd had to take the veil for her support of Eleanor. Yet at this time she couldn't but recall Edith must have plotted with her mother to keep her away from Tristram.

"I remember that, on my wedding night, you didn't deem my husband at all unable to claim his rights. I wonder... Was it you who spread the ugly rumours when I petitioned for the annulment? And was it you behind the forged letter which stated the Church had unbound me from Tristram?"

Her aunt cast her a guileless look.

"Whatever do you mean?"

"Tristram saw the letter, and so did his cousin. And so did Lord FitzRolf. He has it now," Judith said in a calm, quiet voice.

"FitzRolf?" her aunt asked and her voice strived to appear unconcerned, yet Judith did not fail to catch the note of deep worry in it.

"Aye, the very same. And now I'm off to see how my mother fares," Judith said calmly.

Edith was however still lingering and barring her way through the cloister.

"So this is how it is? You seek to abandon your family and to sell us to our foes. You have betrayed our cause!" Edith cried.

"Nay," Judith countered calmly. "The cause was already lost and I accepted our defeat. The treachery is all your own. I doubt Queen Eleanor or your late husband ever knew of your plots. Whatever befalls you, you've brought upon your own head."

Judith strode away, without sparing Edith another glance. When she at last came to look upon her mother, she found Lady Fenice in her cell, which appeared to be more like a lady's chamber than like convent quarters. Her mother was busily embroidering upon an altar cloth, and as soon as Judith entered, she beckoned her to show her the fineness of her work, as if she and Judith had not been parted at all during the last days.

"You've always been the most skilful of embroiderers," Judith said, kissing her mother's cheek.

She then attempted to tell her mother of her journey, and ask her how she fared, yet for a long while Lady Fenice refused to speak of such matters, as if she'd been residing in the convent already for long years. Judith at first began to fear her mother's mind had become even more troubled by the recent events that had passed. At last Lady Fenice spoke to her of the way things truly lay, "I have not taken the veil yet and perchance I will never do so. The Prioress told me there is no need to if I do not wish it. Of course, she has not openly required it, yet it is custom that a gift of money is made to the Priory so I may remain here. I trust your lord husband will make a generous contribution befitting of our rank, now that King Henry has made us destitute."

"We are not destitute! Redmore is still our home, and Tristram will never keep from us what used to be ours. He has wealth of his own and has never in truth craved more."

Lady Fenice waved her hand and made a snort of derision.

"However you may wish to deceive yourself, daughter! Yet I will have him pay a princely sum for me to spend my remaining years here, whether I take the veil or not!"

"Don't you wish to come back to Redmore?" Judith pleaded, still anguished that her sick mother would choose to spend her life away from the home she'd known for so many years.

Her mother shook her head in a determined gesture.

"My sister is here, and several other like-minded women. There is nothing I have to go back to at Redmore!"

Nothing... Judith bit back a sigh, knowing her mother was now angry with her for what she perceived as a betrayal.

"You'll always have a home at Redmore, if you but wish to come back," she said in a gentle voice, hoping her mother would hear the caring in it.

Lady Fenice gave a short, hollow laugh.

"It will not be I who comes back, but you who joins this place sooner than you may think. I am certain the fiend will soon get tired of toying with you and will show his true colours."

"Why do you hate Tristram so? He's never been but gracious to you!"

Lady Fenice didn't choose to answer, but stared away from her daughter, at the cross on the wall.

"Oh," Judith said softly after a while, full of chagrin. "I see. Perchance I was mistaken, perhaps it is not even that you believe me unworthy of his love. Perchance you were always afraid I have found someone I care for more than I do for you. But, Mother, it's a very different kind of love, as you must know!"

"Oh, such brash, uncouth words! You're getting to be more like your father every day! You're... common!" Lady Fenice spat, and Judith's heart clenched in pain at her mother's scorn, but she hid it as she took her leave.

Tristram glanced at Judith searchingly when at last they mounted their horses to leave the priory behind.

"You seem distressed. Do you still fear this is not a good place for your mother?"

Judith shook her head. She had promised herself never to hide things from her husband ever again, and she would eventually reveal to him how her mother had fuelled her own fears and doubts regarding their marriage, yet she would do so in her own time. By then, she hoped her mother would have already found at least a measure of peace and even happiness in the place she'd chosen. And she fervently hoped one day Lady Fenice would get healthy and wise enough to learn to rejoice her only daughter had already found her own happiness.

"No. I'm at peace. Let us go home!" Judith said, casting her husband a warm smile.

R. R. VANE

I discovered romance in a shop which sold used books when I was a teen and I have been writing romance novels in my head ever since. My first ever draft was a medieval romance with a gray-eyed knight, and I still want to finish it one day. For me writing is a dream come true and I always try to stay true to my dreams. So I write historical/paranormal/fantasy romance. My first book (*A Deep Dark Call,* published as Rose Vane) is a Gothic romance set in nineteenth-century Romania. *A Stern Knight for My Lady* is the first medieval romance I ever published.

Visit her website here:
https://rosevane.com/

Don't miss these exciting titles by R. R. Vane and Blushing Books!

Her Stern Husband Series
A Stern Lord for My Lady
The Blacksmith's Woman
Lord Tristram's Love Match

BLUSHING BOOKS

Blushing Books is the oldest eBook publisher on the web. We've been running websites that publish steamy romance and erotica since 1999, and we have been selling eBooks since 2003. We have free and promotional offerings that change weekly, so please do visit us at http://www.blushingbooks.com/free.

BLUSHING BOOKS NEWSLETTER

Please join the Blushing Books newsletter
to receive updates & special promotional offers.
You can also join by using your mobile phone:
Just text BLUSHING to 22828.

Every month, one new sign up via text messaging will receive a
$25.00 Amazon gift card, so sign up today!